A Remarkable Case of Burglary

London 1871. The rich man in his castle, or at least in his substantial Bayswater villa; the poor man at his gate, casing the joint. For many of the poor, crime represented the only chance of a start in life, and ostentatious wealth the temptation to crime. In an era when the police force was still emergent and the telephone not thought of, a wave of burglaries terrorized the well-to-do. It was more than enough to put ideas into the head of Val Leary, Irish labourer. He lacked the tools, the expertise, the capital, but the Soho underworld, then as now, could provide all those. Only before he could acquire underworld backing Val needed an inside contact. And that was where Janey came in.

Janey was the kitchenmaid, the humblest of the servants, subject to the cook, the butler and beyond them the Master and Mistress, whose power to dismiss without a character amounted almost to power of life and death. Through her and Val and a rich range of splendidly realized characters, H. R. F. Keating portrays both the upstairs/downstairs world with its personalities and problems, and the careful underworld preparation of a crime. And in both it is the fallible human element which builds up the suspense to breaking-point and contributes to a totally surprising result.

Temporarily, but only temporarily, deserting Inspector Ghote and India, H. R. F. Keating has applied his talent for making the distant vivid to a time removed rather than a place removed. In doing so he tells a gripping story, recreates a fascinating way of life, and asks some pointed questions about chance and character and the effect of one on the other.

Crime Novels:

BATS FLY UP FOR INSPECTOR GHOTE
INSPECTOR GHOTE TRUSTS THE HEART
INSPECTOR GHOTE GOES BY TRAIN
INSPECTOR GHOTE BREAKS AN EGG
INSPECTOR GHOTE PLAYS A JOKER
INSPECTOR GHOTE HUNTS THE PEACOCK
INSPECTOR GHOTE CAUGHT IN MESHES
INSPECTOR GHOTE'S GOOD CRUSADE
IS SKIN DEEP, IS FATAL
THE PERFECT MURDER
(The first Inspector Ghote novel)
DEATH OF A FAT GOD
THE DOG IT WAS THAT DIED
A RUSH ON THE ULTIMATE
ZEN THERE WAS MURDER
DEATH AND THE VISITING FIREMEN

Novels:

THE STRONG MAN
THE UNDERSIDE

Non-fiction

MURDER MUST APPETIZE

A Remarkable Case of Burglary

H. R. F. Keating

The Crime Club
Collins, 14 St James's Place, London

William Collins Sons & Co Ltd
London . Glasgow . Sydney · Auckland
Toronto · Johannesburg

First published 1975

© H. R. F. Keating, 1975

ISBN 0 00 231712 5

Set in Intertype Baskerville
Made and Printed in Great Britain by
William Collins Sons & Co Ltd Glasgow

'A remarkable case of burglary was committed in a dwelling-house in —— about twelve months ago, and was effected in this manner. One day . . .'

Those That Will Not Work, Vol. IV of *London Labour and the London Poor* by Henry Mayhew (1812-1887)

CHAPTER I

IT BEGAN by purest chance. Early on the first day of
April 1871 Val Leary, tramping in search of work across
West London from the hovel he called home to the new
buildings of Notting Dale, was just lifted out of his
slogging head-down walk by a sharp sound in the still air.
A block of hearthstone was being vigorously scraped on the
steps of the corner house of a street called Northbourne
Park Villas, No 53.

Val's glance rested momentarily on the kneeling maid-
servant on the steps, forerunner of the whole tribe who
would be busy before long outside every house in this
solidly respectable area. It rested momentarily, and then
a second later it returned to her. Perhaps what brought it
back was the fleeting ray of pale sun that caught an
auburn curl escaping from the jammed-on white cap.
Perhaps it was the merest hint in the thin back swinging
awkwardly this way and that of a new-emerging pride in
the swell of the hips. But, whatever it was, Val's glance
stayed resting on the girl he guessed to be a good three or
four years younger than himself, probably barely seventeen.

Then after he had stood there on the far side of the
road for perhaps a quarter of a minute, taking in the girl's
blue print dress, more than a little pulled out of shape with
constant wear, her sacking apron and her patched boots
projecting into the air from where she knelt, the slaty-blue
eyes in his thin pale face narrowed suddenly. His glance
moved up to the house beyond her. With purpose.

The steps being turned an unblemished milky-white

by the action of that block of powdered stone and pipeclay
led to a substantial black-painted front door, its brasswork
already shining with a ferocious glitter. This stood in
a porch supported by two fat white pillars, its roof form-
ing part of the balcony that ran the full width of the house
protected by stout bellying-out iron railings. Behind these
glinted and gleamed three broad sash-windows, their well-
polished panes reflecting the bright first sunshine. Then
above rose two more floors, each with its glinting complement of broad windows growing step by step less in
height. And finally, just visible behind an overhang, came
a last set of windows, for the attic bedrooms, altogether
smaller, hardly measuring two foot square. The whole
front of the house was freshly white-painted and up it ran
in gleaming black four thick waterspouts.

For several separate seconds Val looked at these last, his
eyes slowly travelling up and down them, savouring
each solid foot almost as if they were a repast spread out to
be eaten. And then a look of decision flicked on to his
pale features.

He set off walking again. But now, crossing the road, he
headed down Northbourne Park Villas itself on the pavement running directly outside No 53. His footsteps sounded
louder and louder in the morning air.

Janey, kitchen-maid at No 53, her head down at her
hearthstoning, the harsh rasp of the block loud in her ears,
hardly took in the approaching footsteps. But when,
directly behind her, they ceased with all the suddenness of
a column of soldiers brought to a slammed halt, then the
abrupt cessation of sound penetrated her mind at once. Her
scrubbing stopped. From under her bent arm she looked
backwards to the street.

She saw, standing on the pavement exactly outside the narrow house gate, a young man marked by the greyness of his face as one of the poorest of the poor. His jacket and trousers were wretched cotton fustian, worn and sweat-stained, with patches on both knees and a triangular unmended rip on one sleeve. But the pallid face with the colourless lips was singularly striking under its crown of dark hair, only half hidden by the greasy cap. And the slaty-blue eyes danced with beckoning confidence.

Janey, to her tumbling-over astonishment, found she longed for nothing other than to take needle and thread, run down to the pavement and set to work on that ripped sleeve. But she said nothing and moved not an inch.

Nor did the young man say a word. And, after a few long seconds, Janey turned her head again and started once more to scrub at the step beneath her.

But gone was the steady rhythm of a minute or so earlier, and of day upon day before seemingly almost without number. Instead she found she could do no more than attack the step in little aimless jerks. And beneath the gaze that she knew was steadily on her she shifted her knees uneasily.

At last, when not much more than half a minute had passed, though to Janey it had seemed a whole long morning, the still watcher broke his silence.

He broke it, but hardly broke it. In the stillness, above the hesitant rasping of the hearthstone, there came one single sound. A little click of the tongue, quiet but carrying. A sound such as a horse-coper might make at the sight of a fancied animal.

Janey's scrubbing ceased again. She took her hands from the step, straightened her back, turned and looked at the young man fully and frankly. A smile, a little subdued by caution but ready to ride out into the unexplored world, began to part her lips.

And at that instant, with a clatter that sounded in the cone of intentness that spread from the steps down to the pavement like a rippling explosion, the kitchenmaid from No 51 heaved open the door in the sunken area in front of the house and barged her way out laden with wooden pail slopping with water, long sweeping-broom and awkward box full of brushes and rags and polishes.

At once Janey swung back round, seized her hearth-stone and began furiously scrubbing once more, regardless of the fact that she was whitening a section of the steps already entirely free of every last yesterday's blemish. Only from the corner of her eye did she see the handsome young man in the wretched ragged clothes turn on his heel and lounge off along the wide respectable street, an alien figure.

If chance brings about many events in the world, many more are produced by its opposite, regularity. And the household at No 53 Northbourne Park Villas was a model of regularity. So Janey from the moment she had finished her work on the steps had no time at all to think about the encounter that had so unexpectedly broken the grey pattern of her life. She had to give the back-stairs their daily wash so that every last random heel-mark was obliterated from them. She had to lay the breakfast table in the servants' hall – a salt-cellar at each corner – and then to cook the bacon and eggs and make the tea and be certain it all was ready sharp by half past eight, the later wintertime breakfast hour that would go on till the first of May. And then, no sooner had she eaten her share of the meal, listening all the while to a harangue from Mrs Vickers, the cook, than it was time to clear the table and wash the dishes so as to have the scullery clear and herself tidy before Family Prayers.

But when the whole household was at last assembled in the dining-room for that daily ceremony Janey did have time to think. Usually while the Master sonorously declaimed a passage from the Bible she stood, head bent in a mere daze, recovering from the rush of the morning hardly thinking coherent thoughts at all. But today, as soon as that loud voice began uttering the long words, her mind turned at once to the event that had so startlingly broken in on the unvarying pattern. And from the moment that she conjured up in her recollection the picture of the young man with the dancing slaty-blue eyes – she could see him in every detail clearly as if he were standing beside the Master looking over his shoulder at the big white pages of the fine-leaved Bible – from that moment on her brain seemed to leap and race over a course that had all along been laid out for her, a smooth wide downward-running course sweet and easy to the feet.

That wordless encounter in the morning stillness from being a small nugget of time with neither past behind it nor future in front of it became the starting-point of a whole beaded rope of rich possibilities. What would happen next exactly, she could not decide. But that things would happen, one after the other, getting better and better, more wildly heart-thumping at each advance, she knew with every dumb certainty that was in her. He would come again, her dark handsome admirer. Because admire her he did. That was certain. She knew it from his eyes, from the set of his head, from above all, that tiny little, almost too quiet to be heard but wonderfully carrying click of sound that had come from his nearly-smiling lips. He

admired her. And he would come again. There were the
starting fixed points. And after them all was uncertainty,
wonderful uncertainty in an unfathomable, never before
visited, hardly before thought of realm.

So, when Prayers were done and her duties by Mrs
Vickers's side sending up family breakfast at last com-
pleted and Robert, the footman, and Maggie, the housemaid had come down to the scullery with their loads of
dirty plates and cups and dishes and Robert had dumped
his into the steaming sudsy sink and had hurried off, this
first opportunity of pouring everything out to a sympathetic
ear was beyond possibility of resisting. And out it all came,
every detail as it seemed engraved on her mind from the
instant the ringing steps behind her on the pavement
outside had stopped so suddenly till the moment when the
crash and clatter of that stupid Betsy from next door
had brought to a sudden end the enchanted encounter.

'But he'll come again, Maggie, I know 'e will,' she concluded.

Maggie, raw, red-nosed, lank-haired, gawky of body,
some seven years older than Janey and her only friend in
the world, gave a prolonged sniff of over-dramatic disbelief.

'No,' Janey protested, picking a plate out of the hot
water in the sink and propping it to dry hardly realizing
what she was doing. 'No, he'll come all right. I know
it, Mag. I knows it in every bone in me body. If 'e don't
come termorrer, it'll be because 'e can't. But then he'll come
the next day, or the next. That I know.'

Maggie, slowly beginning to unload the greasy dishes
from her tray, could keep up her hard-won pretence of
superiority no longer.

'What you say 'e looked like again?' she inquired, her eyes beginning to shine in lumbering sympathy. 'What you say?'

Janey sighed deeply and in pure joy. She consulted once more that ever-vivid picture in her mind's eye.

'Blue eyes,' she said. 'A sort o' dark blue, getting on for grey. An' black 'air. Very black. The 'andsomest 'air I ever seen.'

Maggie took the last items from her tray and shook herself out of her uncritical admiration like a dog emerging all-wet from a warm pool.

'Blue eyes,' she said in suddenly heavy tones. 'Blue eyes an' black 'air.'

'Maggie!'

It was Rosa, the Mistress's lady's-maid. Her sharp voice in an instant split wide the intimate cosiness of the warm suds-smelling scullery. Rosa, a proud creature becoming every day more fragile and friable as the years mounted up and there was never a sign of that ultimate seal of womanly success, the husband. The fine complexion beginning to turn papery, the piled golden hair becoming thin and dry, the once-bright voice turning shrill.

'Maggie, there's their bed still to be made, and you standing here gossiping. Come along, can't you? I shan't get a stitch of mending done this morning if you go on at this rate. Not a stitch.'

'Coming, Rosa, coming,' Maggie said, with a pleading grin. 'I was only just a-going to – '

'Never mind what you was only just. Come along now. Come along, do.'

'Yes, Rosa.'

Red-faced lumpy Maggie heaved a great sigh and turned to go. But what she had been just on the point of saying was evidently of such importance that even the flashing imperious presence of Rosa could not quite stop her giving it voice.

At the scullery door she turned and brought it out.

'Blue eyes,' she said. 'Black 'air. That's Irish. Irish, my girl. Irish, so you watch out.'

That evening of April the first Val Leary, who after his early morning encounter had no longer thought it necessary to look for work on the new building in Notting Dale, set out once again from the tumbledown cottage near Lisson Grove, one room of which was all the domestic security he had ever known. He walked down past the Paddington Station and on along to the Marble Arch. But his pace now was not the resigned slog it had been in the morning when all that had been in prospect was a hard day's labour for perhaps as little as eighteen pence in wages. He walked now with his head up and his eyes darting sharply here and there. In Oxford Street, where the shopmen were beginning to put up the shutters and the lamplighter was slowly making his way from post to post, he looked in at those windows that were not yet covered over with quick appraising glances, as if at last he could begin to think about the fine goods they held.

More than half-way down the broad thoroughfare he turned into Wardour Street and some way along that he branched off yet again into a narrow ill-lit lane, not much more than an alley, called Newel Street. Almost the only illumination here now came from the half-curtained windows of a low-built gin-shop, and into this Val went.

Inside, he stood warily just past the threshold, taking in everything there was to see, the dull metal-topped bar, the row of tapped barrels behind it, the pewter pots and

measures and the nets of bright lemons hanging underneath, the sawdusted floor, the three or four rough tables
and the half-barrel seats and three-legged stools, none of
them at present occupied. Last of all he looked carefully
at the two yellow-jacketed carpenters, the only customers,
leaning against the bar, glasses of Old Tom gin in their
hands.

Satisfied that there was nothing untoward, at last he
crossed over to the bar and spoke to the potboy behind it in
a voice so low it was almost a whisper.

'Mr Sproggs at home by chance?'

The thin white-faced lad gave him a quick hard look.

'What'd you be a-wanting with 'im?'

'Business,' Val answered, returning look for look.

'Ain't never seen you in 'ere afore.'

'No,' Val said. 'You ain't.'

He hesitated a moment.

'Jem Walker told me,' he added.

A flash of understanding, quickly suppressed, passed
over the potboy's drawn features.

'I'll go an' see.'

He turned and slid through a narrow curtained doorway behind him. Val stood quite still looking down at the
dented and whorled surface of the bar, the record of
countless haphazard crashings and bangings of pewter pots.

It was three long minutes before the potboy came back.
When he did so, without a word he opened the half-door
underneath the bar.

Val paused for the merest instant and then ducked
through and slipped in his turn through the narrow doorway behind.

He found himself in a little snug room all lined with
dark cupboards and with its sole window firmly shuttered.

The air was redolent with the odour of hot gin and lemon. A neatly cheerful little fire burned in the grate with a black kettle singing on the hob, and the only other light came from a small oil-lamp on a round table in the centre of the room.

At this table, in the sole chair drawn up to it, a comfortable wooden-armed piece of furniture, there was seated a round well-fleshed man of about fifty, who at first and immediate sight put Val in mind of nothing so much as a heavy white-skinned toad. He sat squarely and dumpily in his chair with his elbows resting on the table in front of him, his pale podgy hands clasping a little steaming glass of gin. Beside him on the gleaming dark teak of the table stood a black bottle, squat as himself, and half a lemon and a small sharp wooden-handled knife on a large white plate. His face was white and round as the plate beside him, crowned by a scatter of short brush-like grey-white hair and hardly marked at all by a podgy nose, a small tight-lipped mouth and eyes that under the scanty grey eyebrows blinked a gooseberry-green.

Val was conscious of receiving an unwavering inspection as he came into the room and stood at the near side of the round table. And it was a long while before he was addressed, in a voice so breathily hoarse it was hard to hear even in the quiet all round.

'Jem Walker sent yer. So yer say.'

Val swallowed.

'Not so much sent, Mr Sproggs, as told,' he said. 'Told me where you was to be found, and what the game were you was in.'

The toad-face in front of him flushed up in quick anger.

'What game? What game, eh? Very free with his talk, Jem Walker.'

'I'm a good friend of his, Mr Sproggs,' Val said quickly. 'Honest I am. Not one word o' what he said'll go a yard further by me. That I promise.'

'Hmph.'

Again Val felt himself subjected to a bitterly suspicious scrutiny from the gooseberry-green softly blinking eyes. And again the silence was broken with solid reluctance.

'An' what did 'e tell yer, Jem Walker?'

Val hesitated an instant, and then brought it out.

'He said as 'ow you was a putter-up, Mr Sproggs. He said as 'ow if a likely lad knew of a toffken easy to bust an' worth the bustin', you was the one as'd stake 'im out and provide the companions as was necessary.'

'He said all that, did he?'

Again Val had to withstand a glare that seemed intent on tearing to pieces the holder of such dangerous information. But when the hoarsely whispering voice spoke again it seemed one degree less heavy with suspicion.

'An' you're such a likely lad, eh? Is that the way the wind lies?'

'It is, sir. It is. It come to me only this mornin'. A piece o' luck it was. A rare piece o' luck. I happened by chance to be walking along a road called Northbourne Park Villas. It's just over by – '

'I knows, lad. Noll Sproggs makes it 'is business to know pretty well all the best streets o' London.'

'Yes, Mr Sproggs. Then you'll have seen the 'ouses there?'

'Not me, lad. Never.'

The quick flush of rage came up again on the pale toad features and as quickly died away.

'Not me, lad. It's more'n my life's worth to be seen within a mile o' any place where there's going to be a bust.

B

I ain't never been quodded yet, not fer so much as a day. An' believe you me, boy, I don't intend ter be.'

'No, Mr Sproggs. No.'

Val licked at his lips.

'Well then,' he said, 'let me tell yer that this 'ouse in Northbourne Park Villas, No 53 it is, is a big 'un. An' well kep' up. You can see there's plenty o' push spent there every day, if only by the shine on the brass an' the shine on the winders. But this is the best on it, Mr Sproggs, this is the best on it. There's a servant-girl there what's taken a real fancy to me. She's mine fer the beckoning, Mr Sproggs. Maybe I ain't a-spoken so many words with 'er, but she's mine just as soon as I moves me little finger to call 'er.'

He leant forward across the round table and knew that, for all his exaggerating, his eyes were shining with the fervency of pure truth.

'Is it to yer liking, Mr Sproggs?' he burst out hungrily. 'Is it? Say, it is. Say it is, Mr Sproggs.'

Noll Sproggs' heavy toad face remained totally unexpressive.

'This 'ere servant-girl,' he said at last. 'What class o' servant might she be?'

Val had to think. His brain scrambled. And the unmoving putter-up on the far side of the table implacably recorded the delay in answering.

'Yer don't know,' he stolidly challenged at last. 'You're not half so bleedin' friendly with the lass as yer makes out.'

Val's hands, leaning in fists on the edge of the gleaming teak table, tightened till the knuckles were white.

'Listen, I'll be open with yer,' he said, forcing from within himself every least feather-scrap of conviction he could

raise, seeing slipping away instant by instant the chance
that had come to him, the one chance in a million. 'Listen,
Mr Sproggs, I'll tell you the truth. I don't know the girl
so well. I ain't even hardly spoke to 'er.'

The sweat prickled his upper lip as he told the extra lie.

'I ain't hardly spoke to 'er, but I seen the smile she
'ad on 'er face fer me. I seen that, an' I tells yer. It's
on between 'er an' me. It's on, if ever anything was.'

And, to his thumping joy, the squat putter-up, instead of
angrily dismissing him, asked another question.

'Whereabouts yer see 'er then?'

'It was on the front steps there, Mr Sproggs. She was
a-scrubbing of 'em as I 'appened to pass by.'

'Kitchen-maid then, or scullery wench,' the putter-up
said. 'The likes o' her won't see much on the toff part o'
the 'ouse, if she sees any.'

'But she could ask questions o' the other servants like,'
Val pleaded. 'She could find out anything. She'd do it
fer me.'

Noll Sproggs jerked sharply forward in his wooden-armed
chair.

'Now you watch what you're a-doing of, lad,' he
whispered hoarsely. 'Questions to a servant. She begins to
wonder. Confides in one o' the others. Maybe the Cook, if
so be as she's the motherly sort. And then it's upstairs to
the Master. It's call in the detective-officers. It's shadder
yer, lad. Shadder yer every step o' yer way. And then
one fine day it's those damned crushers in Noll Sproggs's
parlour.'

'Mr Sproggs,' Val came back, summoning up entire
candour on to every muscle of his face. 'Mr Sproggs, I
got more sense nor that. I ain't a half-Irish fer nothing, Mr
Sproggs. I can spin a tale wi' the best on 'em. That girl

won't know one bit about it. She'll talk ter me an' tell me, an' not know a thing she's a-doing of. That I promise.'

The toad-squat putter-up took a long lemony pull from the little gin glass he had all along clasped in his podgy white hands.

'Well then, lad,' he said eventually, with dragged-out unwillingness. 'I'll do this fer yer. You can talk to that girl o' yourn. You can talk to 'er all yer wants. An' you can come in 'ere fer a drink one night. No 'arm in coming in 'ere fer a drink.'

The gooseberry-green blinking eyes looked up at Val, deep past plumbing with wariness.

'An' maybe then I'll 'ave a word with yer,' the putter-up said. 'An' maybe as I won't.'

'Thank you, Mr Sproggs,' said Val. 'I truly thank you. An' you can be sure, come termorrer morning, I'll be talking to that girl o' mine. Talking to 'er fine.'

Scouts make reports. A chief-of-staff assesses them. He weighs factors, allows for chances, seizes on a small lucky event, ponders the forces at his disposal for the attack, adds up their weaknesses and their strengths, bides his time.

CHAPTER II

THE GENERAL-OFFICER commanding a fortress-town takes his precautions, even in piping times of peace. And if on occasion these precautions are strengthened purely by chance they yet keep the enemy at bay. So the fact that on the morning of April the second, 1871, Mortimer Johnson Esq., City merchant and householder at No 53 Northbourne Park Villas, London West, happened while in the act of shaving himself to nick the very edge of the lobe of his left ear was to prove a matter of unexpected importance.

The trivial accident seemed at first to be going to have no more effect than to provide Mr Johnson with a Providence-given chance to vent an ill-temper seldom far below the surface. Temper indeed was, it almost always seemed, the final outcome of the man. He was a powerfully-built aggressive specimen, an inch over six foot in height, notably upstanding and particularly florid-complexioned, the result of fifty years of good eating and more than thirty of measuredly-liberal drinking. He believed to the core that the circumstances of his birth, as a gentleman and as the inheritor of a worthy fortune, entitled him to this good living, as they equally entitled him to exercise to the full the power that had come into his hands. He did not like to be crossed. And when he was so, by the perversity of the people around him either in his household or among the scratching clerks on their high stools at his office in the City, and even by the less accountable perversity of mere fate, he would inevitably break out into a rage which he never considered other than as perfectly just.

So on this morning of April the second, partly because he had always preferred to wield the flashing ivory-handled razor himself rather than entrust his night's growth of beard to the ministrations of Robert, that tiny cut appeared on the lobe of his left ear. And then he felt himself completely permitted to give free rein to temper.

The moment that Robert entered the dressing-room to turn the under-linen warming on the clothes-horse in front of the newly-lit spluttering fire Mr Johnson hastily but thunderingly accused him of bringing up his pot of shaving water 'cold as dead mutton.' Robert, as usual, merely murmured apologies, then quickly spread the linen out again and retreated.

But the incident, and the bluster and haranguing that went with it, had served to delay Mr Johnson not a little in the ritual of his rising. And, in the way of things, this short initial delay built up in little matters like the contrariness of collar-studs, until he was a full ten minutes past his time coming down to take Family Prayers.

And even here he felt himself thwarted at every turn. It was his custom while the domestic staff assembled in the dining-room each morning to glance at the passage of Scripture he was to read – the Gospels were doled out in regular rotation, as had been his father's way before him – and to decide where he could conveniently bring the reading to an end. But this morning he was the last to enter the room, and, eager to make up for lost time, he simply opened the large Bible at the place its broad red-silk bookmark indicated and began to read. And there was nowhere for him to stop.

On and on he went till at last in sheer fury he left off bang in the middle of the Sermon on the Mount, trenchantly pronouncing the by chance somewhat inappropriate words 'pray to thy Father which is in secret; and thy Father which seeth in secret shall reward thee openly.' And then he closed the pages of the Good Book with a single thunderous slam.

Breakfast, with its steaming sideboard array of silver-dished kidneys, eggs and bacon and sea-evoking haddock, with its hot toast, its smoothly-ironed and well-folded *Morning Post* and its substantial pile of reassuring corres-pondence waiting to be opened, gradually mellowed him. But it was a calm that, when broken, was to bring all the more violent a tempest. And before long broken it was. Although when the meal began the teapot was in its place at the lower end of the long table, the tall silver coffee-pot that ought to have stood beside it was not. And, while Mr Johnston sometimes took tea and sometimes coffee according to whim, when he observed along the length of the table that the coffee-pot was not where it ought to be at once he opted irrevocably that day not to drink tea.

And then he sat there, neither eating, nor looking at the paper, nor opening his letters, but drumming his fingers in silent foreboding impatience on the damask cloth and glowering into space while the minutes passed.

The fact of the matter was that the fire in the kitchen-range was sulking dismally and the second kettle would not come to the boil. And for the sulking fire Janey was to blame.

She too, like the Master of the house, had had a contrary start to her day. She had got up promptly enough when the battered alarm-clock had shrilled out at the wintertime hour of half past five in the low-ceilinged chill attic room she shared with Maggie, and she had encountered no difficulties with her first task of clearing out the dead fire from the range and cleaning the flues. But when she had come to light the new fire her troubles had begun. The eight sticks of her allowance for this task turned out to be damp and the two sheets of the *Morning Post* of a fortnight earlier had failed to ignite them. Nor had the sticks caught when she had taken another two sheets, and one extra.

At last she had helped herself to a little lamp-paraffin, a thing strictly forbidden by Mr Burch, the butler. Nevertheless she had at least got the fire to go, if smokily. And though Robert had contrived to bring the small amount of water needed for the Master's shaving-pot to the boil, she herself had not thought to put on the breakfast kettles a little earlier than usual. The kettle for the tea, which was the smaller of the two, had boiled in time. But the kettle for the coffee had not quite been ready when they had come down from Prayers.

And Janey's day had continued to go badly after this partial defeat. It may well have been that her mind was not wholly on her work. The prospect of hearthstoning the front steps, and what she expected to happen then, had already made her forget the evening before to put her sticks down by the range to dry. And so when she came to see to the fire in the servants' hall she had fared no better, and even though she resorted at once to the lamp-paraffin after the first failure, already she was beginning to get well behind time.

Then she found that not only had she forgotten to dry the sticks the night before but she had also forgotten to put her black-leading rag to soak. So when she came to clean and black the front of the range, a task she was meant to perform while coaxing into sturdy life the fire there and keeping an eye on the one on the servants' hall, she found the rag so stiffly board-like that she was totally unable to push it into the whorls and twirls of the decoration on the range and could not even get much of a shine on the flat parts. What Mrs Vickers would say when she came to look at it closely she did not dare think. And, of course, wrestling with the stiff rag had caused her to neglect the already sulky fire even more.

So, eventually, up above in the breakfast-room the Master was left glaring into space and drumming his fingers on the tablecloth while waiting for his coffee. And earlier in the kitchen, immediately after dealing with the range, Janey had found, when at last she seized broom and box and filled her pail, that she was nearly a quarter of an hour later than her usual early time in going out to the front steps. And, as she had feared and dreaded, already Betsy from next door and one or two of the other maids were out at work on their steps. She looked up and down the street. But all she saw was the whisk of a dark shadow disappearing at the far end, too quickly for her to be truly sure that it was really her dark Irish dream chap.

It was a full twenty minutes after Mr Johnson's usual hour of ten that day when Burch bowed him out of his front door, draped in immaculate black surtout, superlatively brushed tall silk-hat on head. By then his customary thorough perusal of the *Morning Post*, which he had declined to abate by a single half-minute, had restored something of his calm. But again it was a precarious calm, all the readier to change instantly into roaring storm for the outbursts that had preceded it. And, because he was twenty minutes after his time, just as he stepped out into the chilly damp air – the brisk weather of the day before had yielded once more to the last dull malice of winter – his ears were at that moment affronted by the sound from the area just below him, of Maggie, his housemaid, in raucous conversation with the visiting ice-man.

Your garrison must have provisions. So it cannot but have links with the people of the countryside around. An Englishman's castle home had to admit the tradesmen.

One of the tradesmen into whose regular round fell No 53 Northbourne Park Villas was the ice-man, a creaking rheumy individual with hands perpetually chapped and raw from loading the big blocks from the ice-pits on to his little donkey-cart. He had too a face as rough-hewn as one of those blocks itself, singled out, perhaps because of the cold he dealt in, by a nose that was an altogether notable large lump of squashy blue.

Yet, despite his awkwardly unprepossessing appearance, Maggie had long cherished for him feelings that were yearningly romantic-cum-practical. Possibly his very ugliness had first sown the seed in her mind. Certainly she used often to make such remarks as 'I dunno, who'd 'ave a girl like me what's more a church doorpost nor a lass beyond compare'. Carefully month after month she had found new remarks to make to him, extracting from him pieces of personal history, chief among them the golden fact that he was, as she had hoped and guessed, unmarried, and had led him bit by bit into her wide-mouthed net.

So she had been ready and waiting this Tuesday morning for his knock, only a little put out by the fact that Mrs Vickers had told her that with no orders for dinner-party ice-creams no ice was needed. But she had contrived not to answer directly her bachelor friend's invariable greeting of 'Any old ice?' Instead she had blurted out a quick 'Hullo, it's nice to see a bit o' sun again,' despite the returned grey winter chill. And from that hasty and long-meditated introduction she had gone straight into the tale of a murderer who had been apprehended on a particularly sunny summer's day, a version of Thomas Hood's ever-popular 'Eugene Aram' culled from the *Servants' Magazine*, one of the few joys of her hard and humdrum life.

The ice-man had listened entranced, open-mouthed. Until, like the thunder voice of a god from the heavens above, the angry tones of Mr Mortimer Johnson, standing on the front steps over their heads, had abruptly cut the saga short.

'What in heaven's name is going on down there?'

Mr Johnson, peering redder-faced than ever down into the area, found that his first burst of simple indignation at the undignified occurrence taking place outside his own house had moved at once by leaps and bounds into altogether more serious considerations.

As he had awaited chastened apologies from below, the remembrance of a conversation he had happened to have at his club some three or four evenings earlier came back to him. Sir Hervey Chalmers of the Home Office had been discoursing to a small circle of chance listeners about the newly-gathered statistics for criminal offences in the Metropolis. And he had had some startling facts to impart. The most impressive of them, to Mr Johnson's mind, had been that a majority of the house-burglaries that had occurred in the period under review had been due in the first place to careless talk by the servants of the house.

So now he turned abruptly from his god-like contemplation of the area, swung round and hammered furiously upon his own front door.

Almost immediately it was opened by Burch, who had been restoring to its appointed hook on the hall-stand the fur-soft brush that he had used on his Master's hat.

An impressive piece of humanity, Burch. He might seem to be designed by Nature to fill the office he held. He was the right height, an exact five foot ten inches, not so tall that he would tower over his employers, not so short as to lack a jot of presence. His fifty-odd years had endowed his frame with a becoming rotundness. His face, if it had not been long and dignified at birth – and his father had been a butler before him – had with the years attained the very essence of length and of dignity, set gravely between two grave lengths of grey side-whisker.

His features now were unerringly arranged into the proper mixture of aplomb and concern as he opened the heavy front door again to his Master's hammering.

'Burch, step out here if you please.'

Burch took a galleon-stately step into the chill air.

'Look down there.'

Burch directed his gaze into the area. Maggie was looking up, her mouth wide as a fish's. Beside her the shambling figure of the ice-man was regarding the house wall in a manner so furtive that it truly looked as if he were contemplating hacking his way through it.

'They were conducting a conversation,' Mr Johnson announced. 'A servant and a tradesman in close and lengthy colloquy.'

'Yes, sir,' said Burch. 'I shall speak to them, sir. I shall speak to each one of them, and it will not happen again.'

'It certainly will not, Burch. Do you know what subject is invariably discussed when talk takes place between a servant and a member of the dangerous classes?'

'No, sir,' said Burch, deferentially ignorant.

'Burglary, Burch. Nothing other than burglary. I had it at my Club, from a very high official of the Home Office. Most of the crimes against property that take place day after day all around us spring from nothing more than idle gossiping between servants and the hoi polloi that come to backdoors.'

'Yes, sir,' said Burch.

Mr Johnson plunged his iron regard directly down on to the ice-man. Already reduced to a state of pervading shame, this latter now turned his head yet further away and agitatedly scraped at the foot of the wall beside him with an enormous ankle-jack boot.

'But I will not have it in my establishment, Burch,' declaimed the voice from above. 'I will not have it. In future, if any servant in my employ is seen to be in social intercourse with a tradesman, or with any casual passer-by, then it is instant dismissal. Instant dismissal.'

'Yes, sir,' said Burch.

'But I cannot be kept waiting about here any longer,' Mr Johnson added, in a sudden burst of pure petulance. 'I shall be late at the office. Late. Late.'

And he launched himself down the steps, along the short path between the two trim laurel bushes of the garden and out to where John, the coachman, had long been waiting, balefully eyeing the ice-man's cart and its shaggy little donkey.

Inside a watchful fortress new orders, whether plainly well-conceived or seemingly quite unreasonable, flick with military rapidity from post to post, from gun to gun.

Janey heard about the Master's new edict within an hour of Mr Burch having received it. He had made it his business to go round to each member of the domestic staff to tell them himself. He had, naturally, begun at the top and worked his way down. He had first 'mentioned the matter' to Mrs Vickers, the Cook. Then he had told Rosa, the Mistress's lady's maid, then Robert, the footman-valet, then Maggie, the housemaid, and finally – having decided that John in the stables in the nearby mews was, with his boy, a separate establishment as were the jobbing gardener and his boy – he came to Janey at work in the scullery peeling her way through the big pile of parsnips that were to be boiled for luncheon.

'And I hope you understand, my girl,' he concluded. 'Not a word of idle conversation with anyone who comes to the door, not with the muffin-man in winter nor the watercress-seller when it comes to the summer, not with the rabbit-skin man – just fetch him what skins you've got, take the sixpence or the ninepence he offers and think yourself lucky – not with the feathers-buyer, not with the man coming for the bottles, nor the old woman who comes for corks. Not with a single one of them. Not the grocer calling for orders – if Cook gives you a message for him, it's tell him straight, say good day and close the door sharp – not with the greengrocer, the butcher, the oilman, the fishmonger. Not with a single soul.'

'No, Mr Burch.'

'Yes, Mr Burch.'

'No, Mr Burch.'

Janey trotted out her replies. But all the while inside, where in the painful years that she had been in the house she had learnt to keep thoughts that were not acceptable, she seethed. Why, why had this order come like this from above on the day, the very day, that it chanced to mean something to her? Two days earlier and she would have listened and hardly taken any notice. Not many of the callers at the kitchen door ever had more than a word for her. The old woman who bought corks might wheedle a bit, but she knew that there was nothing to be got from talking to a kitchen-maid barely out of being a child. And so it had been with the others. But not now. Now ringing footsteps on the pavement had stopped suddenly at the gate. Now a young man with blue-grey eyes and the hand-somest dark head of hair she had ever seen had looked at her and smiled at her. Now in the still morning air a little click of sound had sent a message that said more than a thousand words to her. Now it mattered.

Mr Burch turned, as always as if he had a set of little castors under his well-polished black boots, and left.

And, digging her knife into the tough pale yellow parsnips, Janey vowed she would take no notice of what he had said. Why should she? It was her life she had got to live. She was doing no harm. Only wanting to talk. Talk to a chap. Her chap. And tomorrow she would talk to him, and they could do what they liked. He would come tomorrow. The dark shape at the far end of the road this morning had been him.

And tomorrow she would be out there in time, before all the noseys came out on their steps, and he would be there. He would say something to her. And then she would say something back. And then . . . And then . . .

But sharply, as if a slow ominous thunder-cloud had been building up at the back of her mind, the cold douch-ing shower fell.

What if she was seen talking, and if she got 'the sack'? Instant dismissal, Mr Burch had said. No character to take away with her. Not another position to be found anywhere after that. What have you been doing, girl, they would ask her. And what could she say? What else but work could a girl of seventeen have been doing? And if she tried to tell them about some situation she had been in, it would be 'Well, let me see your letter then, my dear'. And that would be that. 'Out you go, you impertinent creature.'

And as for going back home. Ma had had the two more since she had come here. There wouldn't even be room now, let alone enough to eat. Not room to lay herself down.

But the parsnips . . . She'd never get them done at this rate. And Cook . . .

Yet a few minutes later she had contrived to work herself back into a mood of hope. After all, she told herself, it was always early when she went out to do the steps. Only Maggie and Robert were up and about at that time. And Maggie wouldn't tell on her. Nor would Robert really. It'd mean a whole lot of trouble for him, and he'd never do anything that meant that. Besides, there was only the breakfast-room and the dining-room where anyone in the house could really see her from. And no one would have occasion to go into either of them, unless it was Robert a bit early with the laying of the breakfast table.

So perhaps it was all right after all. But what if she was seen though?

All day the debate raged within her, swinging now this way, now that. While she was doing the potatoes, while she was stirring the caper sauce to go with the mutton, while she was seeing to their own cold dinner, while she was laying the table in the servants' hall, while she was serving their meal, whenever she had time to think she thought either one way or the other. And on it went in the short time that she was eating, and while she was washing up afterwards, their own things first quickly and then those from the dining-room with care. All during the afternoon while she was making the bread, during the long kneading when she was free to let her thoughts run, and again when she began on the vegetables for upstairs dinner, eight courses with guests coming tonight, the two arguments fought for victory in her mind. And the issue remained undecided while she was busy at Cook's side during the long two hours of silence which she insisted on while the difficult business of the dinner was in full bustle. Still while she washed up again afterwards, and on to when she made Cook's and Mr Burch's cocoa for them, she swung from one side to the other. And even when at last she lay on her lumpy flock mattress there was still no victory to either contestant.

First she would think once again of the inexorable facts. She could not lose her position. If it ceased to be, as it could in a terribly short time, no longer than would be needed to be hurried upstairs by Mr Burch to con-front the Master, to hear his thunderous words, to toil her way up to her room and pack her few possessions, then beyond there would be nothing. She could not even see what she would do. How would she live? What would she have to eat? Her few shillings of savings would be gone in no time. And then what? Nothing. Nothing at all. Only to lie down where she was and to die.

But no sooner had she reached this point and resolved that she dare not risk that fate, than, rising to the surface like a growing water-plant in a lake, there would assert itself the golden argument of her nature. There would come into her mind that handsome pallid Irish face, as if its owner were there standing in front of her once again, with his dark hair – and she could see the very way it pushed

C

up from his forehead – with his slate-blue beckoning eyes. He would be there. And she would be unable to deny him.

Only sleep, coming swiftly at last to her narrow bed, ended the argument. And it ended it inconclusively.

Yet the moment the clacking old alarm-clock sounded out next morning she realized that her mind was at last finally and unchangeably made up. She flung her two thin blankets back with a vigour quite unlike her usual reluctance to abandon the slight warmth of her bed. She flung them back. This was a morning when she must not get behind-hand with her work by even as much as a minute. She was going to see him. She was going to talk to him. And no one was going to be there to watch them. Somehow. No one.

CHAPTER III

MILITARY CONFRONTATIONS should be all decision. Facts
appraised, action decided, orders given, orders carried
out. But since confrontations take place in the world there
intervenes between the decision and the action the drift of
chance.

The morning of April the third was one of the ones on
which Miss Christopher, governess to Master Frederick
Johnson, happened to wake early. And, as always when
something disturbed her fragile sleep, she found she could
not lie in bed till her customary rising hour of half past
seven. Anxieties at once invaded her, and even before the
shrill of the servants' alarm-clock, which sometimes she
heard through the ceiling from the attics above, she had
got up and had begun to clothe herself in the black silk
dress that she wore from one year's end to the next, not
letting herself see the way the seams were becoming more
and more visible with each accidental strain on them or the
way the patches of shinyness were being gradually extended
by the casual knocks and rubs of everyday life.

And, as she pinned on the little fob-watch that kept
time so uncertainly, her one piece of jewellery, the worry
that had been foremost in her mind broke through again
like a gnawing mouse. Those scissors, had she or had she
not left them on the table in the schoolroom? From the
moment she had wakened she had seen them, sometimes
there on the table, sometimes in their proper place in the
locked cupboard. Of course she had tidied the room
last night after Master Frederick was in bed. She always

did. But sometimes she missed something. Sometimes, in the most curious and upsetting fashion, she missed the thing that was most under her eyes. And when she did, it was always something dangerous.

Little Frederick might so easily have woken up early too. He was a boy, and boys did that. And, though he was forbidden to leave his bed till she went in to him, he was not always obedient.

Was that her fault? Perhaps it was. She must strive to be more strict. He had to learn. They all had to learn.

He might be in the schoolroom now. Her fingers fumbled at the buttons on the cuffs of her dress, the part she always left till last because the buttons were so stiff. For a moment she thought of running across into the schoolroom with them undone. No one was likely to see her. But suppose one of the servants . . . And it was so important never to be otherwise than properly attired. It lowered one to be seen in public not *comme il faut*. And she could not let herself be lowered.

She struggled with the buttons.

But what if Frederick had got up before he should have done? He might well have gone into the schoolroom – such a pity not to call it the nursery still when Frederick was not eight yet, but it had been decided and it must be – and if he had gone in he was bound to have noticed the scissors. And if he saw them he would take them up. And he would put out his eye. He would put out his eye.

She left the last button on the right wrist, the hardest one to manage, and ran in awkward constrained half-strides into the schoolroom across the landing.

Of course the scissors were in the cupboard all along. And there was no sign of Frederick.

Back in her room she read, not one of the novels of

Miss Yonge that were her secret delight, but, since it was the morning, Mr Bateson's French Grammar. And before long she began to feel hungry.

The onset of the pangs – and they were real pangs, swift, uncontrollable and painful movements inside her – filled her with sharp dismay. Once they had begun, she knew they would not cease. She would not be able to conquer the urge to acquire, somehow, something to eat, something sweet. She would do what she had done too many times before, go down to the breakfast-room, hope to find the table laid and take – no, steal – a lump of sugar from one of the bowls. Or two lumps.

She forced herself to memorize irregular verbs. But she knew them all already.

And then at last, not looking at her unreliable watch, she got up abruptly from her hard chair and made a headlong rush for the door.

Janey was making marvellously swift progress out on the steps. She had been nearly ten minutes earlier than even her usually early time in sweeping them down, and already she had cleaned the big brass knob in the centre of the wide front door and the keyhole. All that remained was the letter-box. And then there would come the hearth-stoning.

She leant forward, in a gesture repeated to the nearest quarter-inch every single morning, to give a final breath-ing-over to the polished brass of the box before the last rub with the soft rag. Her brass always gleamed as brightly as any in the whole Villas, and she was proud of it.

But it had only been by sticking to her exact routine to the hair's breadth that she had kept going. With every second that had passed without the young Irishman appearing she had almost run back into the shelter of the house and to safety from the wild danger into which she had put herself. The thought of what could so easily happen if he did come up and talk to her and if they were then seen, hung in the back of her mind like a yellowy fog, curling and licking. Only by keeping her fingers unflaggingly busy had she fought it back.

And then, unexpectedly for all that she had expected and expected nothing else, it came. Softly from behind her in the morning air a tiny little caressing click of sound.

She whirled round, her fingers nervelessly letting fall the soft brass-polishing rag.

And there he was, just as she had thought of him over and over again all during the last long forty-eight hours. Her heart thudded wildly in the birdcage of her ribs.

'It's you,' she said in one long sigh, as if all her being was melting into a single soft flow.

He smiled without a word.

Miss Christopher, looking neither to left nor right, as if by not seeming to search for anybody she could make sure that nobody would be there to see her, glided across the hall and into the breakfast-room. Swishingly she brushed the heavy mahogany door closed behind her. And onyl when it clicked softly shut did she realize that the long table still had its tan-coloured baize cloth on it and that she must be altogether too early for Robert to have come in and begun laying, even though at least he had already opened back the shutters from in front of the windows.

She looked blankly out at the morning street, still and deserted.

Then she turned to leave. It would not be pleasant if Robert should chance to come in now to get on with his task and find her there. It had happened before, and, though he had always simply held the door open for her to pass through without saying a word, she would feel herself at a loss for an explanation. Of course, she would owe Robert none. But he would know she had been there. And her esteem in his eyes would slip a little more. Which must not be allowed to happen.

Then, as her hand was on the knob, she heard on the far side steps that could only be Robert's. He must be coming in, coming with the big damask cloth over his arm and his baize-lined basket of cutlery in his hand.

She turned and hurried round the big table towards the window with a vague notion in her head of being discovered looking idly out. It would constitute some sort of reason for being in the breakfast-room at this extraordinarily early hour.

Barely four or five yards distant from Miss Christopher's hurrying figure, though separated from her by the solid thickness of the house wall, outside on the steps Janey stood, leaning a little forward, eyes wide and raindrop-bright, listening to the caressing half-Irish voice of the young man who had told her his name was Val.

'Gawd,' she said to him, 'I been scared. The Master, he took it into 'is 'ead only yesterday to say if any servant was a-seen talking to a stranger it'd be instant dismissal. The sack.'

'What?'

The slaty-blue Irish eyes hardened instantly.

'Listen, girl, yer gets time off, doesn't yer? When's that? When is it?'

'My afternoon off? It's termorrer. It's Thursdays.'

The hard eyes glinted.

'Then – Then where'll we say? Kensington Gardens. Yer knows Kensington Gardens?'

'Yes, yes.'

'By the gate there, first you come to in the Bayswater Road. I'll be waitin'.'

'Yes. Oh yes.'

Already he had turned and was making his way off. Sauntering seemingly, but getting over the stones of the pavement at a pace.

'Three o'clock,' Janey called, not daring to raise her voice much. 'Three. I couldn't be sooner.'

In the breakfast-room Miss Christopher, ears tuned to an altogether unaccustomed acuteness by the embarrassment of her predicament, heard in the hall the steps that must be Robert's hesitate. Hesitate, stop, and then recede.

He must have forgotten something, she thought at once, turning from the window out of which she had been for a few moments sightlessly staring. And quickly, so as to be ready the moment he had gone back into the kitchen regions, she swooped round the table and towards the door again.

So in dawn-mist scouts and patrols pass within yards of each other on their probing expeditions, each in blank ignorance of the other's presence. But such hazards are of little account as, in the rear, the two staffs prepare and plan for the coming encounter.

That evening Noll Sproggs, in the guarded privacy of the snug little parlour behind his gin-shop in Newel Street,

Soho, handed his new young Irish acquaintance three separate pennies, passing them across one by one as if they
were taken with reluctance from a small and fast-diminish-
ing hoard. The lad had pleaded that he had to have
something to tide him over till he met his servant-girl in
Kensington Gardens next day, and the putter-up had in the
end paid out.

But when the lad had vanished back through the bar
and out of the house, Noll Sproggs began to hum a little
tune to himself in an unfeignedly contented manner. Little
enough had happened and no doubt it would be long
before he had very much to go on, but an affair like this
ought to move slowly. And if he had made an investment
with so far no return for it, well, he had not parted with
much and before all was done there ought to be rich
dividends indeed.

He helped himself to a not ungenerous tot of the gin
that he kept specially in one of the cupboards lining the
little room, the gin that had not been cut for serving in
the bar. But as the evening was chilly, he did add from the
kettle steaming on the hob just enough boiling water to
make the tipple cheering.

At No 53 Northbourne Park Villas at very nearly that
same time Mr Mortimer Johnson, sitting in his library
surrounded by all the books a gentleman should have in
tall glass-fronted cupboards all round the walls, with
slippered feet comfortably on a well-padded footstool, a large
and cheerful fire burning before him, also came to the
conclusion that the chilliness of the evening beyond
the room's heavy curtains merited a warming concoction.

He pushed himself out of his chair, went across and
tugged the bell-rope, a broad band matching the deep red

of the curtains and heavily embroidered by his wife's own hands. Gratifyingly quickly the door opened discreetly and Burch appeared carrying, in anticipation of the request, a large silver tray on which there rested a decanter of brandy, a single sparklingly polished glass, a long silver spoon and a neat silver kettle on a little stand.

'Ah, Burch, yes, hot brandy-and-water, if you please.'

Mr Johnson, seated again in his deeply padded armchair, watched while the ceremony of preparation was gone through. Then, glass in hand, he spoke.

'Do not go, Burch. I have something to say.'

'Yes, sir?'

Burch bent forward one inch and slightly inclined his grave grey-whiskered face.

'I have been giving some consideration, Burch, to the matter of burglary.'

'Yes, sir.'

'I am disturbed, Burch. Deeply disturbed. Partly on account of the alarming facts I learnt quite by chance at the Club the other day, and partly on account of that disgraceful incident with the girl Margaret yesterday morning.'

'Yes, sir. I have spoken to her. Most severely.'

'So I should hope, Burch. So I should hope.'

Mr Johnson glared down at the cheerful fire in front of him as if it were the offender herself who perhaps deserved after all more than a mere admonition from a butler. But eventually he turned to Burch again.

'So,' he said, 'I had a further word at the Club last evening with Sir Hervey Chalmers, and as a result I have decided to institute extra precautions against intruders. I am right, am I not, in supposing that only the outer doors of the house are locked by night?'

'Yes, sir,' Burch said. 'I make it my business to see to it myself last thing, when I go round making sure the windows and shutters are secured.'

'Yes, yes, man. But in future I want all the doors of this floor and down on the ground floor to be locked as well. They are good stout mahogany, and Sir Hervey informs me that it is a considerable deterrent to a burglar to find he has locks to overcome inside a house when he is in imminent peril of creating noise.'

'Indeed, sir.'

'Very well. See to it.'

'Yes, sir.'

Burch made his way towards the heavy door that would from now on be one of the ones he would make it his business to lock each night.

'Yes, Burch,' Mr Johnson said as he reached it. 'Locks. Locks are the answer. What is well locked up cannot be made away with.'

'Yer does ask some funny things,' Janey said next afternoon as she walked with Val among the smartly uniformed soldiers and the nursemaids pushing their three-wheeled perambulators in the briskly chilly sunshine of Kensington Gardens. 'What yer want ter know what doors is locked in the 'ouse for?'

'Ach, I was only talking,' Val said in answer. 'Sure, I want ter know about the locks on the doors at your place. An' I want ter know about the floors and the tables and the chairs and every blessed thing there is there. An' do you know why?'

Janey could not help laughing.

'You're a funny one all right,' she said. 'I can't think why you'd want ter know all those. The floors.'

Val put a hand on her elbow and brought her to a halt. He looked down at her.

'It's because you tread on them floors,' he said.

Janey's unsuspecting heart gave one great thump. And it was several moments before she could recover herself and pretend to take what he had said half as a joke so as to put something between her defenceless self and this power that had such a laying-open effect on her.

Luckily, so she thought, Val turned to other things and began talking about the gentry briskly walking along the broader paths of the Gardens on this not very warm spring afternoon, the ladies in their fine dresses of salmon pink, eau-de-Nil green and peacock blue, the little boys in their sailor suits or knickerbockers, their small sisters in replicas often of their mothers' dresses if not so sweepingly long, the gentlemen in tall silk hats and elegant frock-coats, bearded and dignified.

Val seemed to have a sharp grudge against them all, a feeling quite new to Janey. She was a little disturbed by it, failing to find here the harmony with him that she had already decided ought to exist in everything between them.

'Ah,' he said at the sight of one particularly portly gentleman with a flashing eyeglass on a broad black ribbon disappearing into an immense beard, 'wouldn't I like to see the wind catch hold of his old hat. I'd like ter see him trot, so I would.'

'No, Val,' she said, filled with a swift uneasiness though hardly even knowing what it was that had caused her to protest.

He made no reply and they walked on in silence. Janey's head was full of the thought of the way in which Val had spoken about the fat gentleman. She felt she would not have been dismayed herself if the wind had indeed taken his hat. She would probably even have giggled when he had set off to chase it. But there was something about Val's way of talking about him that she still did not feel was right.

The silence lengthened. At last Janey, thinking about the gentry at No 53 and all their concerns, broke it by saying that she must be getting back.

'Why, I thought you servant-girls got till evening when you had time off,' Val said.

'Oh, we do, we do,' she answered, quick to defend her sisters in bondage. 'It's only as I've never much to do when I gets out, and no money to spend, I generally go back early. Another time I'll stay till ten. Ten's my time.'

Somehow she felt she could not admit to gentry-jeering Val that the real reason she was constrained to go back this early was because Master Frederick had always insisted that she and no one else made his nightly cup of hot milk and cinnamon.

And so she parted from Val. But he had promised to meet her again at the same place and the same time the following Thursday and as she walked away her whole being was alive with excitement. Yet she nurtured within her her little nut of secrecy.

CHAPTER IV

VAL, FEELING HIMSELF crammed with information about the life and the layout of No 53 almost past remembering, was not too dismayed that Janey had left him earlier than he had expected. He could hardly wait to get to Noll Sproggs's gin-shop and spill out to the wary putter-up all the titbits of knowledge he had garnered. But he encountered a disappointment when he got to Newel Street. The potboy told him as soon as he approached the bar that the guv'nor was out and would not be back till close on ten.

He sensed that his presence all evening in the gin-shop would not be welcomed by the putter-up and so wandered out into the chilly April night. For an hour or more he walked the streets, going over in his mind everything that Janey had said to him, sometimes thinking of their meeting in a week's time and occasionally reflecting that Janey herself had proved to be a bonus he had not wholly expected when the idea of going to Noll Sproggs had first come to him.

But at last the night chill thoroughly penetrated his wretched fustian clothes and his legs began to feel leadenly weary from much walking. He was by now at the far eastern end of Oxford Street and suddenly the thought of the big gin-palaces of Seven Dials nearby at the hub of the no-man's-land rookery of St Giles began to attract him unbearably. He had the price of half a pint of porter in his pocket, if no more, and the notion of using that as entrance money to the dark and thrusting rookery, where at night no policeman dared go unless he was one of a strong raiding-party, became overwhelming.

He quickened his steps and soon the garish cross-roads of the Seven Dials was there before him, its seven narrow meeting roads and its seven flaring gas-lit gin-palaces. Pavements and cobbled streets were alive with people, poor like himself every one, and almost every one of them too plainly sharing his fixed contempt for the prosperous world on the other side of the tall buildings that so stiffly masked this patch of open cut-throatedness.

His pale face took on a little curling persistent smile. Here he felt at home.

He lounged his way through the throng of sharp-faced men and openly brazen bareheaded women, the sellers of cheap goods, the beggars, the whores, the song-patterers with their bundles of ha'penny ballads, the swaggeringly confident sporting types in velveteen jackets happily proclaiming themselves thieves or gulling magsmen. The hoarse competitive cries of the shopmen, ready to sell for what they could get, ready to cheat where they could, were a lapping music to his ears – 'Buy yer ol' clo' 'ere',' 'Hi, hi, the rosy meat at tuppence ha'penny,' ' 'Ere's a fine flannel perricoat, who'll give me sixpence?', and from the dark brown-eyed Jews 'Capth and thlipperth, capth and thlipperth.'

Almost at random he chose the Whiffler to drink his half-pint in. And so by chance upon chance he set eyes almost an hour later, when his pot of porter had only half an inch of tepid much swilled-round drink left in it, on the girl.

There was something about her, as she jostled her way to the crowded bar under the bright glare of the big four-branched gaslights, that seemed to flash an electric message straight to him. She was a coster-girl, to judge by the short skirt that came barely below her mid-calf, by her lack of any bonnet and by the rich brightness of the shawl across her shoulders, and she was probably much his own age. She was dark like himself, and she was pretty with her confident flashing eyes and her sleekly oiled hair. But he had seen girls by the score every bit as pretty. So what was it that had sent that flash through him at the mere glimpse of her? Whatever it was, there was, he knew, a rich chance challenge in the easy movement of her well-set body, a way of walking that signalled to him of sweeping hills under soft rain and the long strides that would pace over them, for all that he had never in his life been more than three or four miles beyond his hovel home in Lisson Grove.

At once he left the crude bench in a corner, where he had rested content ever since he had bought his drink, and moved across towards the bar as if he were a ferry-boat on the end of a long chain being hauled smoothly to a farther bank. He was so quick in getting there indeed that he was well in time to hear her order herself a rum-and-milk and to realize with delight that she was, as he had half-guessed, Irish like himself.

He firmly pushed himself into a place beside her. He had had as he forced his way in not the least idea of what he was going to do or say. But no sooner had he wedged himself in place than he saw what his game must be. He thrust forward the elbow nearest her, holding his pewter pot in that hand. And with an ease that was ridiculous he contrived to cause her to jog his jutting arm and even to spill a drop or two of the small puddle of drink at the bottom of the pot.

At once he wheeled on her and flung out a curse.

And she as quickly retaliated, not with an oath, but with a broad grin.

So he grinned back, as pleased that she had detected his ruse as she had been to detect it. And from that moment they took to each other, like two boiling turbulent streams rushing into the same course, meeting and mingling, till before ten minutes had passed it seemed they had known each other all their lives.

He told her everything about himself, just as it came into his head, with of course all the dark hopes he was pinning on the affair at No 53 Northbourne Park Villas. And, tossed like a thin dried stick in the bouncing flood, there disappeared then, in an unnoticed moment, that first stirring of attraction he had felt for little Janey.

That went. But what did not go, what grew doubly strong in the wild exchanges of confidence, was his determination to use Janey and the power he knew that he had over her to its very last dregs. He told Eileen — Eileen was her name, he had discovered it in the first rush of friendly boxer-blows — that there was a servant-girl at No 53 who was giving him information and that through her at last he would lift himself out of the clinging mire that he had been born into. But he was careful then, and it was the only moment when he did not pour himself out unchecked, to let it be understood that Janey was younger by a good deal than she was, that he treated her in the way a big brother treats his child sister.

He hurried on after this and in seconds they were back to their first extraordinary footing. So together, it had seemed totally natural, when it got near ten o'clock they had made their way out of the roaring jostling whirl of Seven Dials and along to the gin-shop in Newel Street.

They arrived in good time, thanks to Val's now yet

D

keener impatience to hear what Noll Sproggs proposed to do with all that he had learnt. The putter-up himself had not yet retired to his snuggery but was beside the potboy behind the bar, the gooseberry-green eyes in his heavy white face glancing here and there over the customers assessing advantage and disadvantage.

Val went up to him, his sense of being a conqueror strong inside him, and laying a hand familiarly on the dented metal of the bar top, he gave him a broadly cheerful smile.

'Evenin', Mr Sproggs,' he said. 'Here I am. And this is me girl, Eileen.'

He had an instant of foreknowledge in advance of the heavy white-faced putter-up speaking. One instant.

'Get 'er out of 'ere. Get 'er out. An' yerself along with 'er.'

It was savage.

He nearly left without even a protest. But the remnants of the pride he had brought into the crowded sawdust-floored bar made him blabber out some objection.

The putter-up ducked through the half-door under the bar and came close up to him.

'Listen ter me,' he said. 'What was talked on atween you an' me, was a business that was ter go no further. Not one inch.'

And he turned on Eileen a glance of wild suspicion and fury.

'But – But – ' Val stammered.

The putter-up took a heavy step forward, and Val retreated. He saw all his plans, that had seemed to be so firmly on the right path, falling in ruins.

It was Eileen who saved them then. She had been hanging half a pace behind him as he had greeted the putter-up and had stayed there as he had been forced back. Now she darted half-way between them.

'Whist now, I'll go,' she said. 'I'll go directly. Sure, I know well when it's a bit o' business to be talked between two men they don't want no girl hanging round to hear. I'll go this instant.'

She was as good as her word too, making straight for the door into the dark street. Only as she got there did she turn back for a quick moment to Val.

'At the same place then,' she said.

And she was gone.

Her departure seemed a little to placate the putter-up. At least he did not take any further measures to push Val out. And Val, sensing the turning of the tide, began to talk. He kept his voice low and he put all that he knew into it, till at last by wheedling, by promising, by outright lying and by plentiful excusing he managed to induce the putter-up to turn and, with never a word said, lead the way through the bar and into the parlour at the back.

There, not allowed to bring forward one of the chairs that stood up against the cupboard-lined walls of the little room but forced to stand in front of the round central table again like an applicant for a position, he was simply picked apart by the toad-faced putter-up. He was picked apart like a herring being taken off the bone. That was how he put it to himself afterwards.

Far from himself sitting at ease and regaling Noll Sproggs with the whole varied plum-pie of information that he had got out of Janey, as he had seen himself doing, he was instead hoarsely asked question after question as whatever he had learnt was plucked methodically out of him, up one side and down the other.

First it was what the toffken was worth, what the

Master did, whether he kept a carriage, how many servants there were, what jewellery the Mistress had, what notable valuables there were about the house.

'And the plate, lad. What plate they got?'

'Plate?'

So profound was Val's ignorance of the gentry way of life that the word meant nothing to him, and the simpleton question had slipped out before he could bite it back.

'Plate, lad. Silver. How many tea-services they got? How many coffee? What quantity o' salvers? How many table-centres? And candelabra? How many solid silver candelabra locked up there somewheres? And is that in a safe or in a plate-room or in a plate-closet? You find me out all that, lad, an' then I'll tell yer what I think o' the job. Then I'll decide, and not till then.'

And on and on the stripping process went, picking out every chance shred of knowledge that Val had acquired from poor little Janey, who had had nothing but the house that was her world to talk about. After the worth of the place had been assessed, in so far as Val was able to supply answers, the putter-up's hoarse voice moved remorselessly on to ask about the building itself, both inside and out. Val found himself going on a room-by-room inspection, bemusedly discovering that he knew a great deal more than he had ever suspected. He was able to map out more or less what there was on each floor and where at night the sleepers lay, whom at some distant time, if he could persuade Noll Sproggs at last, he himself would be in danger of waking.

'Butler upstairs, is he then? Yer sure o' that? Many a butler's made ter sleep acrost the door of a plate-room.'

'No. I'm sure, Mr Sproggs. Janey said as 'ow he went up ter bed. I call them very words ter mind. Up ter bed.'

'Good, lad, good. An' ter sleep sound on 'is Master's wine what he's helped hisself to an' accounted for as going off, so I hopes. So I hopes. An' now, lad, the outside. What did yer make o' that?'

And the detailed questioning began again, and once more Val found that things he had hardly thought he had seen were of vital importance. He watched the putter-up's heavy toad-head shake sadly when in all innocence he told him that the garden at the back was small and the houses over the way looked right down into it, 'so,' as Janey had said to him, 'yer can see them two great sons o' the place comin' in sometimes at gone five o'clock of a morning just as we're a-getting up, Maggie an' me.'

For a moment then Noll Sproggs had looked down at the dark table-top in front of him.

'Back way's no good then,' he said at last. 'An' back way's best way. Allus remember that. No crushers a-coming on their beat ter see yer, all the time in the world yer wants.'

He sighed heavily. But then he looked up, blinking his gooseberry-green eyes.

'What about the attics?' he asked. 'That Janey o' yourn sleep right under the roof?'

'Why, yes, she does, she does,' Val replied, delighted to have a good solid answer to give. 'She told me. It's blazin' hot in summer under the slates, she said, an' freezin' cold of a winter. Half an inch o' ice on her jug o' washin' water many a time. Half an inch.'

'Yeh.' The putter-up was unsympathetic. 'So slates a-pulled off o' the roof's out. More's the pity. But what about the water-closet? Got a water-closet in the 'ouse, yer said?'

They had. It was Janey's duty to clean it when she

did the back stairs.

'Leave the winder there open of a night? There's some on 'em does that, fer what they calls the 'ygiene. We could put a snakesman in likely.'

'A snakesman?' Val asked before he could stop himself.

'A chavy. A kid. One as'll go through where they don't think as 'ow it's possible.'

'I don't know about whether the winder's left or not.'

'Then find out, lad. Find out.'

And so it went on. After the worth of the place, the layout. And after the layout, the people.

One by one Val had been put through the dwellers in the house, and had had dragged from him all he had been told about them – the Master, the Mistress, the butler, the cook, the lady's maid, the housemaid, the footman and even Janey herself.

'There's no kids then,' Noll Sproggs concluded thoughtfully. 'No nursemaids, no governesses, no kids.'

'No, no, there ain't kids,' Val gave the assurance. 'That there ain't.'

The toad-faced putter-up shook his head briefly.

'There's one blessing,' he grudgingly admitted. 'Kids is the devil on a bust. Always a-waking up in the night. Stomach-ache, bleedin' nightmares, want ter do a wee-wee.'

'Yes, Mr Sproggs.'

Val forced awe into his voice. Nor was it hard. He had had no notion that interrogation in the way he had been questioned for the best part of the past two hours even existed. But, for all that he made himself sound as admiring as he possibly could, it was by no means certain yet that Noll Sproggs would give him the help he would need. And he saw now how much more difficult it was to make a bust like this than he had at all guessed. The thought of trying on his own to get into the house at No 53 and come out with enough to haul him that heavy step out of the mire fluttered like a juddering reed in his insides.

And those gooseberry-green eyes, hard and wary behind the blinking lids, were on him still.

'All right, lad. Here's a deaner fer yer. Come an' see me next Thursday mornin'. Afore yer goes ter that girl o' yourn again. An' I'll 'ave some questions fer yer to keep in mind. A many questions.'

Val took the glinting shilling coin and felt excitement send the blood running in his veins. The way lay open.

CHAPTER V

YET FOR ALL Val's optimism, days went by and days turned into weeks and still the wary putter-up would not fully commit himself. Still the invaders' general was content to push out vedettes by ones and twos, fast-mounted horsemen riding with care round the extreme perimeter of the defences, observing and reporting back.

The money doled out to Val had mounted and mounted, and still every Thursday morning he went to Newel Street and learnt by heart a list of questions that he was to slip into the talk with Janey when they met in Kensington Gardens or as later he took her, a delighted child, to a penny gaff to laugh at the comic songs, to hiss and call out at the silent miming villain and to cheer, her eyes shining, the silent hero and the silent heroine. Getting the answers from her was easy, so easy that occasionally Val felt a twinge of conscience. But he had only to remind himself of what knowing Janey meant to him in the way of a chance to lose for ever the dull gripe of hunger which seemed to be always in his stomach and the clammy clothes that were always on his back. And then at once he was able to jump his mind into being again simply the lad who loved this girl.

Then it was as if the days and nights dabbing it up in the rookery at St Giles with Eileen were happening to someone else in some other existence. His need drove him out of that world and into Janey's, and so long as the need persisted he would be able to live happily in the light of her eyes, eyes that hardly left him from the moment they

met under the trees in Kensington Gardens till the moment
they parted at night not far from the house at Northbourne
Park Villas.

But gulling Janey was not the only task that Noll Sproggs
exacted from Val in return for the grudging supply of
deaners.

For fourteen whole nights in succession he had to stand
in the dark of Northbourne Park Villas, in a narrow niche
between the wall of a house about half-way down the street
and a thick-trunked sycamore tree that had been left growing in the pavement and observe the lamp-lit length of the
road. In his pocket was a watch the putter-up had lent
him, a heavy old repeater in a gun-metal case, though the
last thing Val would do would be to play out its chime.
But every time the policeman on the beat went down the
street – his heavy-booted steps ringing out on the pavement
in the night silence, each one distinct and leaving its tiny
after-sound hovering in the chilling air – Val pulled the
watch from his pocket, clicked it open, held it so that
its face at last caught the dim light from the nearest lamp
and committed to memory the time it said. And there he
waited in his hideyhole until the street showed the very
first signs of stirring to life, and he noted exactly what
happened first and just how early it took place.

For two weeks he kept up this vigil, waiting till within a couple of minutes of the time Janey came out on to
her steps, but never staying to see her. Instead he made
off walking as hard as he could go – with the blood after a
little moving in his veins with the exercise and dispelling
the long cold of the night – until he reached the gin-shop
in Newel Street. And there, early though it still was, Noll
Sproggs would be waiting for him. Two long bolts would
be slipped back on the door at his cautious knock and he

would be admitted to the empty bar to give an account of every incident he had seen since the midnight start of his observation.

By the end of that time Val reckoned that the putter-up knew all there was to be known about Northbourne Park Villas between midnight and dawn. He knew where lights stayed lit till a late hour, where carriages came up to doors long past the time when all the rest of the street was a-bed, where lights suddenly went on in the cold small hours. And, above all, he knew the whole routine of police activities along the street. He knew not only how regular the particular policeman allotted to this beat was – and he was one of the clockwork ones, it seemed – but he knew which night he had off-duty and how his relief kept his watch, which was every bit as regularly.

And then for another week Val was set to follow the beat policeman himself, No 126, as he went on his round. He began the task with some hopes. Noll Sproggs had told him that what he had to look out for was times the fellow would linger somewhere, whether there was a kitchen door at which in the early part of his night he was admitted, whether he stepped just once into some quiet nook and smoked a pipe, whether he took a drink anywhere. But as night followed night and Val went slinking here and there, hands thrust in pockets, lounging and waiting and hurrying on to a next corner, his hopes were slowly extinguished.

Policeman Watson seemed to be a model personage. Regularly as a ponderous clock he kept to his exact routine, passing down each street on his beat every twenty minutes and never once stopping, even surreptitiously to sit down for a brief rest, during the whole eight hours of his duty, 10 p.m. till 6 a.m. On he would go at the same

swinging gait, lifting up his head to stare at the few
night-time passers-by, watching them leadenly until – Val
felt after a little that he could see exactly what was
happening in that heavy mind – he was sure who they
were and what business they were abroad about, and
then turning away and continuing at the same slow tick-
tock pace.

But Noll Sproggs had not been put out when he had got
these reports. On each of the last three mornings on which
he had been given the dispiriting tidings of Policeman
Watson's clock-like regularity Val had almost been prepared to hear a brusque 'so ferget all about it, lad.' But
that had never come. And Val had felt trickle away the
anger he had tried to stoke up in himself, an anger he
wanted to be fierce enough to make him override all the
difficulties that night by night he was coming to see
would stand in the way of carrying out the bust of
No 53 single-handed. He had felt the rage go down with
a relief that almost had him smiling outwardly : he knew
all too well now that anger was not enough for a business
like this though he knew too that if it did not go on with
Noll Sproggs' support he would go on without it. The
aniseed tang of the trail was too sharp in his nostrils for
any going back.

But Noll Sproggs' patience was far longer than Val had
ever dared hope. It extended even to his withdrawing for
all these three weeks the attention he had been devoting
through Val to Janey. Val was to meet her still. But he
was to avoid questions about the house just as much as
he had been made to press them earlier.

'There's been affairs I give up when I'd spent five pound
on 'em an' more, lad,' the putter-up said once. 'Give
up 'cos some servant-girl took fright at the mention o' the

Mistress's jewellery.'

And Val, living and thinking Eileen in St Giles now, his home near Lisson Grove visited only because Noll Sproggs told him it must be in case in some unguessed-at emergency Janey tried to get hold of him there, was relieved that those afternoons in Kensington Gardens were complicated only to the extent that during them he had to make himself forget that he knew any other girl but the one at his side.

Janey, coming late to their meeting place on Thursday, May the twenty-third, was seething with fury against Mrs Vickers. She had been stopped by her just as she had been ready to go, shawl over shoulders and straw bonnet on head, and had been made to scour again with sand and vinegar each of the twelve copper frying-pans, ranging inch by inch down in size, which she had, her thoughts deep in the afternoon ahead, failed to bring to the required pitch of brightness that morning.

But, despite this, despite her longing to pour out all her troubles to Val, to force him to comfort her, she knew at once, the moment that she came up to him, that he was no longer the Val she had left the Thursday before. In the past few weeks he had lost – she had been increasingly sure of this – all the three-parts hidden defensiveness he had had lurking within him in the first days of their love. And she had thought she had known why. The idea he had had, the idea which she never liked to put into words even in her own mind, the idea about the house : he had at last given up. As one week succeeded another and he ceased asking her those questions she refused to think about, she came more and more to believe this. No, it was true : he was not making up to her just to find out all about the house. Maggie, in the talks they had in the dark of their bedroom before sleep overtook them, had been wrong with her hints and suspicions. Val loved her for herself.

And now, without his having said a word, she knew that things were different once again. It must have been something in the way he was standing, or in the way he looked at her as she came up, somehow too glad to see her. He had something to hide, and with an inward sinking she half-guessed what it must be.

But there was nothing she could do about it. She had learnt that much. She had learnt it in the last few weeks without knowing how. There were things that came to you, good things sometimes, bad things more often, and all you could do was to live with them, good or bad. And this was one of the bad things. That she knew too.

So all she could do was to go on as if nothing had changed. She burst out with all her troubles, Mrs Vickers, the pans, how nearly ready she had been to leave, how all she had had to do was to tell Mrs Vickers she was going, how she knew that her tormentor had deliberately waited till that moment before telling her she had seen the way she had done the pans. Out it all came.

'Gawd,' she said. 'One day she'll drive me to murder. That bitch.'

It was a pleasure to use the word. Like driving a knife into something. And the pleasure a little kept at bay the new fear that had come to her from the moment she had seen Val.

'I'd like to murder the bitch,' she said again.

And then she saw the sudden hardening in those slate-blue eyes that she loved.

'Sure,' Val said. 'Nothing'd be too bad for the likes

o' Mrs Vickers. But there's worse than her.'

'Worse?'

'There's them behind her.'

Too late she realized the trap she had walked into. This was that dangerous, down-tearing Val she had heard more than once before and had feared.

'No, Val, no,' she said. 'It is Mrs Vickers. She delights in what she does to me. She delights in it for herself.'

'That's as may be. But when she does, is it to the Mistress you can go to tell your troubles?'

'Oh, Val, no. No, I could never do that.'

The thought of exposing her small concerns before that distant figure was a huge impossibility.

'So then,' Val said, leaning towards her, 'who's at the back of Mrs Vickers when it comes down to it then? Who but them, the gentryfolk there?'

'Yes, but . . .'

Then, as the real truth of what he had been saying struck home, she felt rising inside her a dense black force, compacted of all her suppressed resentments during the long-drawn years she had been 'in service'. It rose. It grew. In moments it blotted out everything else that she had had in her head, that she had come in those past years to accept as unchangeable. And at last it broke out in unsayable words said in the light of day.

'Val. Val. There's no need fer yer ter come over me like that, not no more. I knows why yer wants ter. And – And if there's anything yer wants ter know about No 53, then I'll tell yer. I'll tell yer, Val, ter the last inch.'

She saw him blink in bafflement. The sudden utter revolution within her had been altogether too much for him.

'Val,' she rushed on, 'I knew from the first what you

was asking me all them questions for. I knew it, only I wouldn't let meself think it. I know why yer wants ter know about the 'ouse: it's ter come in, ain't it? It's ter break in? Ter come in an' rob us all?'

She had so leapt on in advance of him that she saw him for an instant considering whether to deny everything. But a moment later he gave her a crooked sort of sideways smile.

'Well, since yer asked . . .'

'But, Val. Val, tell me this. The floors, Val. When yer said that about the floors one day. That you'd been asking about the floors in the 'ouse just because them was the floors I trod on. Yer meant that, didn't yer, Val? Val, yer meant it?'

A half-thought, spinning away from the edge of her mind, told her that she ought not to let him know how easily he could hurt her. But she was past caring.

And, to her swamped relief, he replied to her. Not in words. But by taking her hands in his and looking long and hard into her eyes.

At last it was she herself who answered her own question.

'Ah, Val, I knew it. I knew in my heart yer couldn't 'ave said a thing like that and not meant it true and true. Meant it from deepest down. Oh, Val.'

And after that she had had no hesitation in answering any and every question he chose to ask.

So that evening in Newel Street Val felt, as he sat on a hard chair facing Noll Sproggs in the little snug cupboard-lined back parlour, that he was well able to provide the putter-up with every bit of the new information he had been asked to acquire. And, heading by heading, he went through the list of the possible valuables to be found in the house.

'And the Mistress's jewels, boy?'

'Kep' at the bank, Mr Sproggs, but brought out regular when there's some fine show or other as they're a-going ter.'

The gooseberry-green eyes looked at him with their customary suspiciousness.

'And how's she know that, your Janey? A girl what's only a kitchen-maid?'

But Val was equal to this.

'It's that Rosa,' he answered at once. 'Always a-boasting o' how much she does for the Mistress, an' how much she knows. An' never more so than when the jewels is ter come out. You'd think they was ter go round 'er own neck and to dangle from 'er own ears the way she goes on about 'em, so my Janey says.'

A last look of doubt lingered on the white toad-face.

'Boastful, is she, that Rosa? Then how am I to know she ain't a-boasting o' the jewels? How am I to know they ain't paste, every last one on 'em?'

'The gentry wouldn't be so worried about putting 'em back in the Bank if they was paste, Mr Sproggs,' Val answered. 'Rare old fuss the Master makes about 'em going back next day, Janey says. Wouldn't be so particular if they was snide, would 'e?'

Noll Sproggs grunted.

But Val found to his delight that the next question indicated plainly that the putter-up was advancing the affair steadily in his own mind.

'Your Janey, she know just when the jewels is likely to be brought out? She know beforehand?'

'She do, Mr Sproggs, she do,' Val almost chanted in reply. 'Rosa gets to know an' she tells the rest on 'em soon enough. All over 'em with it she is, every time.'

The white toad-face remained unmoving. To outward appearance.

'Willing enough ter sing, that girl o' yourn,' the putter-up commented grouchily. 'Willing enough. What you done to 'er, eh? An' what's that Irish o' yourn going ter say about it?'

Val avoided this last question, avoided even thinking about it.

'It's not me what's done anything ter Janey,' he answered instead. 'It's that Cook there, that Mrs Vickers. Gone fer the poor dollymop night an' day, she 'as. An' turned 'er right against the whole lot on 'em at the last. Right against 'em every one.'

'An' turned me to it,' said Noll Sproggs. 'Turned me to it in the finality of it all.'

Val, sitting squarely, knees apart, on the hard little chair opposite him, felt a bound of joy and a sudden keen coursing of excitement swinging through and through him.

'You come Saturday, lad,' the putter-up went on the faintest bleam showing in his gooseberry-green eyes, 'an' I'll 'ave Climbing Charlie 'ere ter listen ter yer, Climbing Charlie what's the king-pin o' the whole trade. An' then you'll see. Then you'll see the strength and the breadth of it.'

CHAPTER VI

A GARRISON that sleeps is a garrison open to sudden on-slaught. A prudent garrison commander, or one simply subject to spasms of unaccountable nervousness, will not let his watching troops slumber even when there are no reports of an enemy in all the leagues of country round. Bugle calls will ring out even in the dead of night. Guard parties will be stood to.

'Burch,' said Mr Mortimer Johnson in a rush of in-explicable fretfulness from his legs-apart stance in the library on the night of Saturday, May the twenty-fifth. 'Burch, I will take my nightcap.'

Burch, a slowly inclining pillar of dignity, as he set down the weighty silver salver he had brought in anticipation of this request, looked up from the array of glasses and bottles.

'Yes, sir,' he said. 'A hot toddy, sir. Or whisky and seltzer?'

Mr Johnson sighed.

'Whisky and seltzer, I think,' he answered.

'Yes, sir. A distinctly warmer evening, sir. We shall have full summer upon us before long.'

Mr Johnson stared with gloom at the Turkey carpet before him. The thought of the progress of the seasons, of time passing, oppressed him. He experienced, without being able to bring himself to frame the feeling in words, a sense of the inevitability of things, and the notion contrasted not at all comfortingly with a vision of the transience of human endeavour, even of his own endeavour.

'Burch,' he said with sudden force, making the glass in the butler's hand jerk by the smallest of amounts. 'Burch, I have been thinking. The plate. I am not at all happy about the safety of the plate.'

'No, sir,' Burch said advancing with the filled glass, at once concerned and reassuring.

Mr Johnson took the glass from the salver, soon to be replaced among its fellows, larger and smaller, in the iron-doored, double-locked plate-closet behind its screen in the breakfast-room. He examined the whisky and the trails of seltzer bubbles rising up in it.

'No, Burch,' he said. 'There is only one thing for it. To-morrow I shall set in hand the purchase of a good fowling-piece and a proper quantity of goose-shot. And, Burch, you will sleep in the breakfast-room with this beside you, and loaded.'

'Yes, sir,' said Burch.

He spoke with respect, if not with enthusiasm.

Mr Johnson pondered for a little, still eyeing the tiny lines of bubbles wavering their way to the surface of his glass.

'No,' he said at last. 'No, on second thoughts, that won't answer.'

'No, sir?'

Mr Johnson shot his butler a sharp look. Had there been a hint of relief in the man's tone?

'No,' he said firmly. 'However early you were to rise, Burch, the breakfast-room would be bound to suffer from the presence of a sleeper in it all night. There would be an atmosphere.'

'Yes, sir,' said Burch.

'No. You had better sleep across the way in the dining-room. You will be in easy ear-shot there. Yes, that will do excellently.'

'Yes, sir.'

Mr Johnson regarded the new arrangement with sombre satisfaction. He did not allow to obtrude any thought of the odour of smoked cigar and stale wine in the dining-room that would all too certainly linger on far into the night.

After a little Burch, busy with the array on the salver, ventured a discreet cough.

'There will be the matter of a bed, sir,' he said.

'Bed? Bed? What bed is this?'

'If I am to sleep in the dining-room, sir, it will not be possible to bring down the bedstead from my room each evening.'

'Hmph. Then you had better arrange for the purchase of a camp-bed. Something suitable. A lightweight affair.'

'Yes, sir,' said Burch.

The silver salvers and the candelabra, the glinting table-centres and softly shining tea services at No 53 Northbourne Park Villas were, at this same time, much occupying Val Leary as he walked down Wardour Street towards Noll Sproggs's gin shop for his late-night appointment to meet the notorious Climbing Charlie. Eileen was on his arm, still delighting in spite of their weeks together in holding him and hugging him. The prospect of the meeting, the joy of having at last secured Noll Sproggs's full backing was filling Val with dark and leaping thoughts of at last coming into the world of triumphs.

'In two minutes, Eileen mine,' he said as they reached the turning into Newel Street. 'In two minutes, me love, I'll be talking to Climbing Charlie. An' the three on us'll be thinking o' the way we're a-going to make that bust, Charlie an' me.'

Eileen dragged him to a halt in the light that streamed

from the gas-lit interior of a chandler's shop still serving ounces of ham or Dutch cheese for the late suppers of the ever-wakeful Soho dwellers. She stood half in front of him so that she could clearly see his face.

'An' you're certain sure,' she asked, 'that we'll be rich after?'

'Sure, haven't I told and told you. Old Sproggsie ain't the man to take up an affair unless it's a big 'un. An' if it's big enough fer him, it'll be big enough fer you an' me to have something to live on fer ever after. A little public out in the suburbs maybe, wi' you behind the bar an' me up an' down from the cellar.'

Eileen thrust her face yet nearer his in the diffused light from the chandler's window.

'Me behind the bar?' she jerked out at him, fiercely and abruptly. 'Me? Or her? That skivvy girl o' yourn that you're so close with?'

'Ah, not a bit of it,' he protested with easy assurance. 'Sure, I'm friendly wi' the girl. Sure, I walks out wi' her, an' she takes me arm as we go. But don't I have ter be friendly? Don't the whole bust depend on what I finds out from that dollymop?'

'Is she pretty?'

The question was as fierce as the one before.

For a moment Val was tempted, in this solitary area where his innermost cunning prevented him giving his complete self to Eileen, to deny as brazenly as he could that Janey was in any way pretty. Then better sense, sharper cunning, prevailed.

'Sure an' she's pretty.'

And he watched the temper come flaming up in her, the temper he had only had hints of as yet in the still continuing first haze of love. He watched it come boiling up, and he judged his moment to a nicety.

Just when the scalding words were about to rip out, just as the clawing fingernails were beginning to come up towards his face, he seized her by the wrists.

'Pretty she is, is Janey,' he said, looking down into her eyes. 'But beside you, Eileen mine, she's no more than the butt-end of a candle beside the biggest gas-chandelier o' them all.'

He saw her gasp with pleasure.

The pride sang in him.

'Now,' he said, 'off with yer quick. Old Noll don't like a girl around when there's business to talk, remember. An' I've business tonight that'll last me a lifetime.'

In the attic bedroom which Janey shared with Maggie at No 53, the sloping-ceilinged room with the small square of window partly obscured by the parapet of the tall house, the two of them were talking. Janey was recalling, her face on her thin pillow suffused with pleasure, how her chap had told her that he loved to speak about the very floors she trod on because it was her feet that touched them.

Maggie sighed. For several long moments the little dark room was silent. But at last Maggie palpably abandoned the dream.

'It's more'n floors he talked about, I bet a shilling,' she said. 'He's talked about locks too, ain't he? He's a cracksman, Janey. I know it.'

'No,' Janey protested with what force she could.

'Well, if 'e ain't a cracksman, what's 'e do then?'

'He ain't exactly got no job just now.'

Maggie's voice at its most lugubrious floated up in answer to the boarded ceiling so close above her.

'Then you ferget 'im, me girl. You ferget 'im. My ice-man's a ice-man, if I ever dared be seen a-talking to 'im. But yours is plain danger ahead, that's what yours is. You ferget 'im.'

'I won't,' Janey pledged herself. 'I won't. I can't. Oh, Maggie, I loves 'im. I loves 'im. I'd do anything for 'im, anything in the whole wide world.'

' 'Ere,' said Maggie, suddenly alert. 'Don't you a-go a-doing that.'

She rose up in the dark on one elbow.

'Don't you do that,' she said, relishing her small store of worldly wisdom. 'You only got one lot o' goods in this world, an' you wants ter keep that fer a man as'll marry yer.'

Confused thoughts ran hither and thither in Janey's head as she lay flat on her back in the narrow bed, the mattress hard and lumpy as ever underneath her.

'You wait till you get asked,' she replied defiantly at last. 'You wait afore you comes so free wi' your advice. If that's what I 'ave ter do ter 'old 'im, that's what I'll do. So there.'

And she heaved herself on to her side and shut her eyes tight.

But before long she felt impelled to add something.

'An' besides, I wants ter. I think.'

'Cor,' said Climbing Charlie, leaning right back in his chair at Noll Sproggs's round table. 'Cor, I reckon this lad's skivvy-girl has been a-letting 'im 'ave a bit o' the old bless-me-soul down some little alleyway. 'Cos 'e can't 'ave 'ad much time for asking 'er questions if 'e ain't never found out about the plate-closet door.'

Val felt a hot sense of resentment. Hadn't he done well? Hadn't he done very well? Got more out of Janey than anyone else could have?

He glared across at Charlie. From the very first he had found him not at all what he expected. He was light on his feet all right, you could see him going up a waterspout like a monkey up a tree, or dancing jaunty as an acrobat along some ledge fifty feet above the ground. Yet he had seemed to treat the whole affair as no more than a joke. He had laughed all the time. Even Noll Sproggs, sitting in his usual hunched way with his little glass of gin in front of him, suspicious as a spider, had not been able to stop Charlie making a joke out of every word that was said, his face split at every moment by a wide grin, his pale blue eyes under their sandy lashes always darting here and there, never holding to any one thing for a single moment.

Could he really be the man he was meant to be, the one who would rather climb all the way up the side of a house than go in by a window, the one who delighted in crossing rooftop after rooftop, jumping over gaps that went right down to the ground below, so as to lift the slates from somewhere everyone else had thought could never be touched?

' 'Ere, wake up.'

Val glared at him. But Charlie was only the more amused. That grin, carving his sandy face in two, flashed out once more.

'Go on,' he said. 'Yer must know, boy. Is it a rub-a-dub-dub? Or what is it?'

And all Val could do was to repeat stupidly 'Rub-a-dub-dub?'

'Cor, don't yer know nothing? A rub-a-dub-dub. A Chubb. One o' Mr Chubb's patents. 'Cos if that's what we're a-going to meet on the night, then it's a screwing job, boy, an' not a crack-in. Yer can't crack ol' Mr Chubb's patents, not no more nowadays.'

'I don't know what it is.'

Val cursed himself for having no better answer. But Noll Sproggs had never asked him to find out what sort of a door they had on the plate-closet there, and how was he to have known that was so important?

'Well, you'd better find out, boy.'

For the first time since he had met him Climbing Charlie sounded serious. Serious and exasperated.

'You'd better find out. 'Cos I been done down by plate-room doors afore, I 'ave. An' I don't intend to be done down by one again. If it's a bust what no one ain't been able to see whether it's ter be an easy climb or a stiff, then that's neither one way nor the other ter me. I can do it, boy. Whatever it is. But I'm not going ter go in there an' find I'm cheated by a blasted door. See?"

The putter-up, his white face heavy and unmoving as always, now leant suddenly and sharply forward in his chair.

'You do what 'e says, lad,' he said in his hoarse whisper that was never less menacing for its quietness. 'You do what Charlie says.'

'I'll do me best; I can't do more,' Val retorted, furious at the blame coming to him that ought by rights to have stayed with Noll Sproggs, and unable to risk getting one inch on the wrong side of so powerful a patron.

The putter-up's greenish eyes glinted coldly.

'Listen ter me, me lad,' he said, the hoarse words cutting into the quiet air of the snug little room. 'Listen ter me. I was a-standing at the corner jus' now, taking the air afore yer come in. An' I saw yer. An' that Irish o' yourn. Very friendly you was together. Very affectionate. Well, if yer don't want me to tell that Eileen – it were Eileen, weren't it? – that you're a-tailing that skivvy-girl, then yer finds out all about the plate-closet door there. Yer finds out quick.'

Val felt himself battered by the hoarsely uttered words as if they had been a rain of blows from a heavy stick. That the putter-up had found out so much about him and had remembered every least thing down to Eileen's very name, which he could have hardly heard once, made him feel as if he was laid out in front of him just like the gin-bottle, the glass and white plate with the half-lemon on the table at this moment, with every least nick and angle plain to be seen.

'Yes, Mr Sproggs, yes.'

It was all he could say.

Val recalled the feeling every bit as vividly on the following Thursday night as in the soft darkness with Janey leaning snugglingly on his arm, he found himself nearing just such a dark alleyway as Charlie had jeered about when he had accused him of not having asked about the plate-closet door at No 53. A dart of frustrated anger flicked up in him at the thought that so far Janey had refused all the afternoon and evening to tell him anything about the door.

She was keeping it from him, he knew. Some donkey trick in her was making her keep back the thing he most wanted to hear from her. Why, he was unable to think. She had been willing enough to tell him anything he had thought of asking the Thursday before. Why hold out now? It must be because she thought she could make him surer this way.

But she'd have to find out –

He came to an abrupt halt and swung her round on his arm till they were facing each other.

'Val,' she said, before he could put his question yet again. 'Val, I mustn't linger. I've to be back by ten, yer know.'

'There's time in plenty,' he answered, dropping suddenly into a soft crooning note very different from the one he had meant to take. 'Sure it's not ten minutes easy walking to the house from here. An' we've a full half-hour yet. The church clock's not long struck.'

'Well,' she said, 'a minute then.'

Val licked his lips.

'Janey, love,' he said, putting all the persuasion he knew into it. 'Janey, tell us about that plate-closet door now. What's it look like? Is there writing on it? Is it wood now, or iron?'

'But, Val, I told yer. I ain't never seen it.'

His pent anger broke through.

'You a maid in the house,' he stormed. 'Been there three year and more, and you try saying you ain't never seen that door.'

'But I don't go in the breakfast-room,' she answered, plaintive under his anger. 'I don't go in the gentry part o' the house ever, 'cept for Prayers in the dining-room of a morning. Kitchen's my place. Kitchen an' scullery, up the backstair to bed at night an' out in the morning to scrub the steps.'

But no explanation she offered abated his fury. The thought of Noll Sproggs's white menacing face came back to him loomingly.

'You must 'ave been up there some time,' he said. 'You must ha' done.'

'Well, once or twice a year I gets into the top part o' the

house fer a bit. Like Christmas, when we goes up to get our presents from the Mistress, our cotton dress-lengths. An' I been sent with a message once or twice. But only that.'

He still could not chase away disbelief, though he was more inclined now to put her failure to help him down to some error of hers.

'But ain't yer once been in that breakfast-room,' he said. 'That's what they calls it, ain't it, breakfast-room?'

Janey stood in the dark and thought, biting her lower lip.

'Yes,' she said at last. 'Maybe once, soon after I first come. But the plate-closet's behind a screen there and I didn't never see a bit of it.'

'Still,' Val urged, 'if you been once, you could go again, couldn't yer?'

'I might. I s'pose I could. I will if I can.'

Hope broke through the damped-down sullenness inside him, a quick flicker.

'That's better,' he said. 'I was beginning ter think as you'd gone off o' me.'

'Oh, Val, never. Never.'

He saw her face leaning towards him, pale and ferociously determined.

'Not if,' he asked, with a little half-playful jibe in his voice, 'not if that what's his name, that footman, started a-making up ter yer?'

'Robert,' she came back with sharp scorn. 'If Robert was found passing the time o' day with me, 'e might be set ter work.'

Val pounced at this, the alert beast in him ever ready.

'Yer said that about Robert afore. That 'e does the least 'e can. D'yer think he'd ever leave a bolt on a door not shot?'

'Mr Burch is the one what always sees to the bolts,' Janey said. 'An' you won't find him fergetting a single one, never.'

'Old fool,' Val glinted out.

Janey shifted a little in his grasp.

'Yer can't blame 'im altogether,' she said. 'I'm not sticking up fer 'im, mind. High an' mighty, he is. But he 'as got the Master on 'is tail, night an' day.'

'Still on wi' his locks and locking then, the Master?' Val asked, feeling the beginnings of despondency again.

'Getting worse by the day,' Janey answered. 'An', Val, that's why I ain't sure as 'ow I can ever get ter that plate-closet door for yer. If I was caught in the breakfast-room . . . Val, ain't there no other way?'

'No, there ain't,' he burst out, furiously plunging his grimed fingers into the flesh of her arm.

Then at her little gasp of a cry he relaxed his hold.

'Listen,' he said, almost apologetically. 'There ain't no other way than this bust fer a chap like me ter get a start. An' if I doesn't get ter know about that plate-closet door, there ain't no bust. I can tell yer that.'

The bitterness flooded through him, and he flared out again.

'So you gets in there an' looks at it. Unless yer don't want ter come a-walking with me no more.'

She stepped away from him half a pace.

'But, Val,' she said in an abruptly tear-stained whisper. 'Val, I can't promise. I'd like ter do it. I wants ter do it. Fer you, Val. You. But I can't be sure. I can't.'

She gave a choked half-sob.

'Oh, Val,' she said, 'I loves yer. I loves yer so.'

'Then prove yer does,' he flung back at her. 'Prove it.'

'Val, I will.'

He frowned. There was something about the two words she had uttered that was unexpected. Did they mean she was promising after all to go into that breakfast-room for him? It didn't sound like it. But . . .

'That's more like,' he said cautiously. 'Yer takes yer chance an' hops in there, gets a good look at – '

'No, Val. Val, it's not that. I can't do that if I can't, an' if I can I will. Yer know that. But, Val . . Val, it's something else.'

'What?'

He felt suspicion jut up in him like a hard spike.

'Val, if yer promise not to leave me, if yer promise ter go a-walking wi' me next week an' next an' ever after, whether I got things ter tell yer or not, Val, there's something I will give yer.'

'I don't want none o' yer givings,' he answered sharply, spurning some bribe of a bright-coloured handkerchief or gimcrack tie-pin. 'What I wants is ter know about that door. That an' nothing else.'

'Not what you asked o' me last time?'

It took him several moments to see her meaning. And even then he felt topsy-turvily disconcerted. True enough, he had suggested to her the week before that they should go down into the concealing darkness of this self-same passageway where two high brick walls running the length of the big gardens of two houses and leading to a back entrance to a third made a long trough of dense darkness. But he had not in the least expected her to agree. He had seen it as just one more way of showing her that he was hers, one more strand of rope across to the prisoner ship. But to have his words then taken up like this . . .

'Oh,' he said.

It was all he could find to say.

CHAPTER VII

Mrs Vickers, sitting alone in the servants' hall, back straight as a rod, quite clearly heard the knock on the area door that she knew was Janey's before an instant later the distant bell of St Stephen's Church began to chime out ten o'clock. Her face tightened with rage. The wager with herself which she had been so sure in the last few minutes that she would win had been lost.

The last stroke of ten came echoing in from the night outside. Mrs Vickers bounced to her feet and with quick slicing strides went into the kitchen and across to the area door. She turned the key sharply in its lock and swept the door wide back.

The girl was waiting outside in the dank darkness. Her hand was even raised to knock once more.

Mrs Vickers felt fury shoot out of her.

'So, my girl,' she said. 'Here you are. At last.'

She saw Janey blink in the pale swathe of light coming from the kitchen behind.

'But, yes, Mrs Vickers, I'm 'ere.'

'And I suppose you know what time of night this is?'

A look of swift appalledness on the girl's face was Mrs Vickers' reward. So the chit hadn't been careful to be in on time. Just as she had thought. Out in the dark and not knowing what time it was. Only one thing that meant. Little slut. Little slut.

'But, Mrs Vickers. Mrs Vickers, it's only just done striking ten. And ten o'clock's my time. I was here by then.'

Hussy. Try to get out of it, would she?

'That's as may be, my girl. But ten o'clock's when Mr Burch has to be able to tell the Master the house is locked and bolted and safe. And how can he do that, you young madam, when you're out and about, prowling up to heaven knows what wickedness?'

'But I was here before ten struck, Mrs Vickers. I run all the way.'

And then something in the girl's face, a sudden recollection, a memory of what she had been running from, of who she had been running from, no doubt about it, sent a thrill through Mrs Vickers as if she was a bitch-hound and had suddenly caught the scent of a soft and tender rabbit.

'Don't you dare speak to me like that,' she flung out at Janey, knowing that whatever she said the girl, with the thought ripe in her mind of what had made her so nearly late, would be battered under it. 'Don't you dare contradict me. If I say you were in after ten, after ten you were in.'

'But I wasn't.'

She stood looking down at the girl – a slip of a thing, too young for it, you'd think, only they none of them were, none of them – and she saw the silly creature was holding up her wisp of truth as if that would keep her out of trouble. Oh yes, she might have been at the door by ten. But she shouldn't have been, not after what she'd been doing. She shouldn't have been, and she wouldn't be.

And now the chit was blabbering.

'I wasn't late, Mrs Vickers. I wasn't. I half-killed myself to get here on time, and I did it. I did.'

'You hussy. You stand there and call me a liar to my face. I'll see to you, my girl. I'll see to you. It's up to the Mistress first thing in the morning for you. It's up to the Mistress and she'll have a word or two to say to you.'

She darted a hand forward, seized the girl's wrist, delighting in the power of her well-muscled arm to toss this slip of a creature back and forward, from side to side.

She pushed and jerked her ahead through the kitchen and on to the foot of the backstairs.

'Get up to bed with you,' she ordered, feeling the words ripping like a knife-tip across tender meat. 'I'll do without my cocoa tonight. And you get up to bed, and lucky for you the Master's out at that opera or you'd be up before him now and out of the house ten minutes later. You hussy. You little hussy. You hussy.'

To Janey Mrs Mortimer Johnson was a figure like a goddess. It was very seldom that she saw her, remote and gliding, dressed always, it seemed, perfectly as a picture, in shining satins and brocades in winter, in floating muslin and lace in summer. And when she went out in the evening and wore her jewels. Then Janey always contrived, if it was possible at all, to stand on a chair at the kitchen window and peer up from the area just so as to catch one glimpse round the side of the laurel bushes of the marvel as she stepped into the waiting carriage. Never, of course, had this being from above set foot in the kitchen, Janey's world. Only at ten o'clock each morning would Mrs Vickers go up to her in the drawing-room to get from her the orders for the day's meals, her large slate under her arm.

Janey could almost have counted on the fingers of one hand the number of times the Mistress had actually spoken to her. There had been the summons when she had been 'engaged for the post of kitchen-maid', a process which, in a world so different from the crowded cramped home that had been till then all she had known, had con-

F

fused her to the point of hardly at all understanding what was going on. There had been the Christmases since she had been in the house, when she had gone up to receive those dress-length presents and had had addressed to her the words 'Happy Christmas, Jane' and had replied, after much bullying coaching from Mrs Vickers, 'Happy Christmas, ma'am, and thank you very much indeed.' And that had been all.

She had heard tales of the goddess, of course. Greek peasants long ago heard tales of their deities, some loftily moral, others freely admitting weaknesses shared by ordinary humans. But, though with one part of her mind Janey had accepted that there were human fallibilities in the beings upstairs, whenever she actually caught a glimpse of the Mistress she saw only a figure far above any possible failings.

So just before ten o'clock on the morning of Friday, May the thirty-first, to be trailing up the backstairs in the wake of the stiffly marching, starchily-aproned figure of Mrs Vickers on her way to see that goddess was an ordeal that seemed to damp down the very beating of her heart.

And it was not just to confront that distant figure. It was to suffer her wrath. What would happen to her? What would the Mistress say? What would she do?

Janey was incapable even of framing guesses in answer.

All she could contrive was to repeat one thing to herself, one small piece of practical wisdom that she had been able to hammer out of her panic as she had carried out her morning tasks. 'Call her ma'am. Call her ma'am.' It might a little avert the wrath.

They came to the baize-covered door separating the backstairs at the level of the first floor from the gentry part of the house. Mrs Vickers pushed it open, apparently paying not the least attention to her charge. She had been like that all the morning. As if determined not really to see her.

They crossed the broad landing. The feel of the un-accustomed thick rug under her coarsely-shod feet was for Janey the beginning of losing her bearings altogether.

What would the Mistress say? What would she do? Call her ma'am. Call her ma'am.

Mrs Vickers opened the broad mahogany door in front of her a discreet three or four inches, put her head into the gap, ascertained that there was no reason why she should not enter the drawing-room, swished the door wide and marched forward.

Janey followed, swept along behind, a bobbing, empty, rudderless boat.

The Mistress was standing at the far end of the big, square, light-filled room beside a piece of furniture, tall, curlicued, gleamingly polished, which only later was Janey able to name as a piano. She was holding a sheet of paper, with printing on it that Janey realized dimly was not proper printing and later too decided must have been a sheet of music. Yet she knew somehow – instinct going to the heart of things – that the sheet had been quickly snatched up when the door had begun to open and that it was not being properly looked at now for all that the Mistress, that gowned figure, was holding it in front of her.

'Ma'am,' Mrs Vickers said, advancing across a heavy green and red carpet, 'I've brought Jane to you. I think as you ought to speak to her, ma'am.'

Speak to her. Janey just grasped that this was something much less terrible than the Cook's threats of the night before. Was this the reason she had not given a word to her all morning? Was she going to tell the truth in the end, in spite of everything? And would she herself get off lightly after all?

Janey saw, as if she were watching a figure in a mechanical show through a thick pane of glass, the Mistress put down the square of paper on a round table draped to the ground by a green plush cloth. And she got the impression again that suddenly the goddess had felt that she ought not to have been holding the sheet.

But if the Mistress could not make up her mind what she was meant to be doing . . . ? Janey felt yet another anchor of certainty sheared away.

'To speak with her, Mrs Vickers? Yes. I see. Yes.'

The Mistress suddenly picked up the sheet again from the green-covered table, looked at it as if she did not quite know what it was and then put it abruptly down.

Mrs Vickers gave a little scratchy cough.

'I'm sorry to say, Ma'am,' she announced, 'that Jane was not at home by her time last night. Ten o'clock had struck when I opened the door to her.'

The words had been coming to Janey as if through thick transparent gelatine. So it was an instant or two before their full meaning struck her. But when it did she felt totally helpless. They were the truth. The door had not been opened to her till ten had struck. So how could she fight that?

And what would the Mistress say to it? It was against the rules. Would she be turned away then? Given her month's warning?

'Yes, yes, I see. I see.'

The Mistress did not sound like an avenging figure. But she was far away in the gelatine that Janey felt enveloping the whole of life up here. How could she be appealed to?

'So if you would speak to her, ma'am.'

And it seemed that Mrs Vickers equally felt that the distant figure had to be firmly addressed if she was to respond at all.

But now the Mistress was turning fully to face her. So it was going to come, whatever it would be.

Janey swallowed and felt herself go white, a coldness as the blood withdrew.

'Yes. Well, Jane. Ten o'clock. Ten o'clock is the hour at which you are to be in, is it?'

But surely, Janey thought bemusedly, everybody knows that.

'Yes,' she said. 'Yes, ten.'

'Ten what, Jane?'

The question, in that soft scented voice, was entirely unexpected. And inexplicable.

'Ten what?' Janey repeated. 'Ten o'clock.'

'Jane,' came the soft reproving voice again.

She could only stare round her in bewilderment.

' "Ma'am", Jane. You must always say "ma'am" when you address me.'

Janey felt a sweeping sense of horror. The one thing she had been sure would ward off a really terrible reckoning, and she had forgotten it. She had let fall her lucky charm at the very start, and it was shattered to pieces.

'Yes, ma'am. Yes, ma'am,' she stammered, knowing that it was too late.

'Good, Jane, good.'

But then the Mistress ceased altogether to speak. She turned away and her hand stretched out towards the sheet of paper on the green tablecloth once more. Was she going to say nothing else?

Janey hung suspended.

But with her hand on the paper the Mistress suddenly shied away from it, turned towards her once more and frowned sharply.

'Yes, Jane,' she said, as if she had been talking all the while. 'Yes, what you have done is wrong. Very wrong. And I must reprimand you for it. That is my duty.'

She seemed instant by instant to be getting angrier and angrier. Janey felt increasingly bewildered. That long word, the inconsequence of it all, each pushed her further and further from any shore.

'Yes, Jane, it is disgraceful. Disgraceful. To stay out so late in the night. After ten o'clock. After ten.'

Despite the moment-by-moment pumped-up fury, Janey felt a sudden anger in herself at the sheer falseness of what was being said about her.

'But I wasn't out after ten, I wasn't, I wasn't,' she shouted.

The Mistress stepped back a hasty pace. She looked round as if for help. But then with startling abruptness she launched a wild attack of her own.

'Quiet. Silence. Stop. I will not have this. I will not have it. I never heard such talk. Stop it, stop it this instant. You wild, wicked girl. Go. Go, this minute. Leave the room.'

But Janey was too utterly surprised, too battered and shocked to move.

'I will not have it, I cannot have it.' The tumultuous stream poured down on her still. 'I will not have girls who cannot control themselves. Go, go at once. You're very lucky not to be dismissed out of hand. Go away. This instant. Go away and come to me again tomorrow. When you can control yourself. Yes, tomorrow. When you are calmer. Go. Go.'

And at last Janey took in the meaning of the words

apart from their battering effect. She turned, saw the broad polished door, ran to it, struggled with clammy hands with the knob, induced it at last to turn, hauled the door wide and flung herself out.

More to hide from that unexpected spume of anger than out of any sense of the proprieties she succeeded in catching hold of the door-handle and drawing the heavy mahogany closed behind her.

Then, thankful for this protection, she stood there.

And slowly the dazed bewilderment she had been drowned in ebbed away. To leave a sand-bar of pure resentment. Everything that she had had to push down over the years in which she had been in the house rose up solidly in her mind, all the orders that she had had to obey against her inclinations, all the unfairness that had been idly thrust upon her. The child she had been who had had to learn sharp lessons in a strange world, and had learnt them in silence, now wanted immediate revenge at any cost.

She longed to hit out. To hit back.

And at once she saw how she could do it. The breakfast-room. At this time of day no one was likely to be in it. The family had well finished their long meal. Robert and Maggie had brought the greasy dishes down to her in the scullery before Mrs Vickers had summoned her to go upstairs. Maggie should have finished her sweeping and dusting there easily by this time, and she should too be done in the hall and on the front stairs.

So there would be nothing to prevent her at this moment running across to the backstairs, tumbling down them, emerging again a floor below, making sure that no one unexpected was about and then scurrying quickly across to the door of the breakfast-room, slipping in, hurrying over to the screen, peering round behind it and looking and looking at that plate-closet door till she had got every piece of it pressed into her memory.

And then she would make them suffer. Then, thanks to Val, the lot of them would smart.

The idea had no sooner burst open in her mind than her feet were taking her, on silent tiptoe, across the soft rug of the landing towards the baize door to the backstairs.

She felt those feet of hers tapping and drumming under her down the familiar bare stairs that she scrubbed each day. She felt the baize door into the hall open silently and swishingly before her. She saw the hall empty and echoing as she had known it would be. She felt herself almost gliding across it.

For a moment she checked at the breakfast-room door, so much was it like the door to the drawing-room above where it had been such a terrible moment to wait not so many minutes before. But the anger within her still lay hard and stone-like, and in an instant she had turned the intricately-worked brass knob and had pushed the heavy door back.

And, yes, of course there was no one in the breakfast-room. And at once the whole place came alive from the one half-forgotten time she had seen it months and months before. There was the long broad table with its thick daytime tan-coloured cloth on it. There were the tall leather-seated chairs, ranged up at it. There was the sideboard, gleaming and newly-polished. And there was the screen. The high, heavy screen in stamped leather.

She looked at it for one long hungry second, and then she darted forward. And she was round it. And there, there, was the plate-closet door at last.

It swung abruptly and silently wide. The tall commanding figure of Mr Burch stepped out.

CHAPTER VIII

A TRAITOR TROOPER, in defiance of all orders riding out from the siege lines to pass information to the enemy outliers, a secret transaction under cover of the morning mists, is, as a chance wind boisterously puffs, abruptly revealed. Halt, who goes there?

'What are you doing coming round behind the screen, my girl? Were you coming into the plate-closet?'

Mr Burch's long, decorously whiskered face was gravely suspicious. It seemed to Janey somehow like a bloodhound's, quickly yet calmly hunting from point to point on a trail. On her trail.

'Oh no, Mr Burch,' she blurted out in hot denial. 'No. No, I weren't.'

The butler regarded her with steady scrutiny.

'It looked very much to me as if you were,' he said. 'And what are you doing in the breakfast-room at this hour in any case? One moment while I turn the key in the closet lock, and then I shall want a word with you.'

He swung calmly round to the plate-closet door and a moment later Janey heard the heavy click of the key. Her mind was scrabbling everywhere for a hold. She must find something to say that would be believed. But what? What?

And now the butler had slowly wheeled round again and his solemn questioning face was looking down at her. But then at last the words came.

'Oh, Mr Burch,' she said, a sob coming unbidden into her voice. 'Oh, sir, I come in here to have a good cry.'

But the butler continued to regard her with calm suspicion.

'A breakfast-room is no place for a servant to weep in,' he said, stating a rule.

'Oh no, sir, no. No, I knows that.'

'And what do you have to weep about, my girl?'

'Oh, sir, I was afraid of being turned away. Mrs Vickers took me up to the Mistress, sir. An' she wouldn't hear one word o' what I got to say fer meself.'

The tears flowed now. All her troubles had seemed suddenly to come up in a lump to her throat.

But Mr Burch was shocked.

'Now, none of that,' he said with sharpness. 'I'm not going to have evil-speaking about the Mistress.'

Janey sniffed the flooding tears to some sort of a halt, so strong was the disapproval she felt beaming out at her.

'No, Mr Burch,' she said through a sob. 'No, sir.'

'No, just you remember this, young Janey,' the butler went on, unexpectedly calling her by her name for the first time ever to her knowledge. 'We all of us have to put up with them. They are our Mistress and our Master, and we have a duty to them. Do you think I like having to sleep every night on a canvas bed? Do you think I enjoy it when the Master stands over me making sure I have locked doors and windows that it's no more than my place to do?'

'No, Mr Burch,' Janey whispered, in answer, amazed at revelations.

'I should think not. But I accept it. I accept it, Janey. Or I give in my notice.'

He looked at her with a quick return of shrewdness.

'And it is your duty to do the same,' he said.

'Yes, Mr Burch,' Janey answered. 'Oh yes, sir. But I

don't want ter give in me notice, sir. I darsen't. There's
too many on 'em at home fer me ter go back, sir.'

'Then you had better mind your Ps and Qs, hadn't you?'
the butler replied.

But the words were on a note of dismissal. And Janey,
her heart suddenly bounding as she realised that her
interrogation had ended without any unanswerable question having been put, bobbed a curtsy, turned and scuttled
out of the breakfast-room as fast as she decently could.

In a few scrambled minutes before her midday dinner that
day, Janey, borrowing pen, ink and paper from Maggie,
who every other Sunday solemnly composed an account of
her doings for her parents in the country, set herself the
difficult and unaccustomed task of writing a letter. It was to
Val. Short, direct – and horribly ill-spelt – it told him how
she had tried and failed to get a sight of the plate-closet
door and that she was under threat of the sack next day if
the Mistress was still 'in a taking'. Then she bought a
penny stamp from Mr Burch, telling him that it was
her mother's birthday next day and she wanted to write, and
even got his permission to run down to the pillar-box at the
next corner.

She spent her short dinner-time anxiously asking herself
if the letter would get to Val. Would a postman go into the
lane off Lisson Grove that Val had once described to her?
Did they have more than one delivery in such parts? Would
Val be able to make out what she had written? Had he
ever told her he could read? She was unable to remember.

But she got little time during the rest of the day for
worrying. Mrs Vickers, perhaps because she was thinking
it was her last chance, seemed to be more on her tail than
ever. She was made to spend the afternoon once again

scouring the long descending row of copper frying-pans, with frequent inspections to make sure she was hard at it. During preparations for upstairs dinner, though there were no guests that night and nothing more than the usual six courses to prepare, she was kept doubly on the go.

So only at last, lying in her narrow lumpy bed, did she have time to worry once more. And that was for only minutes. Hardly had she slid between the coarse sheets than, physically exhausted, she was overtaken by deep sleep. And only in dreams was she racked with terrible anxieties, confronted with abysses, left always in doubt.

Next morning she was out on the steps earlier than she had ever been. The kitchen fire, liberally soaked in lamp-paraffin – if that was missed, would she be there to be blamed? – had caught with a quickness it had never before shown. The fire in the servants' hall, belching up thick sooty smoke, had gone equally well. And then there she was, out in the morning sunshine, its fresh pleasantness mocking her, and carrying on with her various tasks as slowly as she could so as to make sure she stretched the time out-of-doors to its utmost in case Val, if he had got the letter, was delayed.

But he was there before half past six, mysteriously appearing round the corner, keeping close to the wall, cap pulled down hard over his eyes, half on his toes ready at a glint of danger to cut and run.

'Janey.'

'Val. Oh, Val. Yer got – '

'Listen. Can't stop. Just listen, Janey.'

'Yes, Val. Oh yes.'

'Listen. When yer sees the Mistress this morning – '

'Oh, Val. What'll she do ter me? Val, if I gets the sack I – '

'Will yer listen. Talk to her, girl. Talk to her good, talk to her soft. Keep that place o' yourn. Keep it. Go on yer knees if yer has to, but keep it.'

But her long-kenneled rebellious spirit had tasted blood the day before, though it had been deprived of the kill.

'Down on me knees? I won't. It was lies Mrs Vickers was telling o' me, an' I ain't a-going to abide by 'em. Not fer no one.'

She saw his slaty eyes harden, even at the distance from the top of the steps to down where he was lurking half-hidden by the gatepost.

'You'll do as yer told, girl. You'll do it, if ever yer wants ter see Val Leary again.'

She felt abruptly sick at the threat, a sudden cold sickness that made her shiver from the small of her back to the nape of her neck.

'But, Val,' she pleaded. 'If it was lies, an' strike me if they weren't, why can't I throw them in 'er face? Why can't I?'

' 'Cos you being in this 'ouse is the only chance I got,' he said, hammering the words quietly in the morning air as if they were so many nails each to be driven home at a blow. ' 'Cos without you in there, it'll all be off, finished, forgotten, never so much as thought on again. That's why.'

'Yes, Val.'

She could not but submit. Here, out here, with him only a few yards away, looking at her with those eyes which she could see at any moment she cared to close her own, speaking to her in the voice she knew to its every last inflection, she could do nothing other than acquiesce totally in his demands.

But even as she did so a tiny insistence in her, far, far away, asked if she would always obey, whether in three or four hours even, when it came to the test, she would be able to rein in that urge that had risen up careless of everything the day before.

A general depends on his chain-of-command. Sectors of the battlefield have to be entrusted to senior officers acting on orders that cannot cover in detail every contingency. To such officers, whatever deficiencies they may happen to have, must be left much of the actual conduct of a defence.

Mrs Mortimer Johnson felt her heart beating fast inside her. She must not betray the nervousness. What would Mortimer think, what would he say to her, if he found out that she became afflicted with such alarm at the mere prospect of dismissing a servant? Dismissal, if it should come to that, was after all no more than her duty, the duty of the Mistress of a household.

She looked, for the twentieth time in the past quarter of an hour, at the gilded clock with its well-fleshed figures of the handmaids of the hours under its thick dome of glass on the overmantel. Nearly ten. And, punctual to the second, Cook would come in with her slate under her arm and the girl trailing behind her. What was her name? Jane. Yes, Jane. And then she would have to reprimand the creature, reprimand her with severity. And what if there was another scene then like yesterday's? If there was she would have to do it. Put the girl out of the house. And it seemed such a cruel thing.

She bit her lower lip.

Mortimer would repeat to her that it was her duty. And duty had to be done. If she failed in it, he would be angry. Justifiably angry.

With a soft whirr the gilded clock chimed the hour, ten purring strokes. And on the tenth the door opened and Cook first put her head round and then came fully into the room. Came sailing into the room. And the girl draggle-tailed behind her.

Mrs Johnson found that her lips and mouth were fiercely dry. She did not feel capable of uttering a sound. But, with tears stinging the backs of her eyes, she commanded herself to speak.

'Good morning, Cook.'

The sound was a fearful croak. But it seemed not to arouse any surprise. And the greeting was returned quite in Cook's customary way.

For a few moments, hoping it really was not longer, Mrs Johnson stood allowing herself to dwell on her dislike of Cook. She had never liked her. But she was a good cook. No, an excellent cook, both in the meals she sent to table and in her running of the kitchen. There was no faulting her. She could not conceivably be dismissed. She could not be as much as rebuked. Oh, if only she would ask for another ten pounds a year. Or fifteen. Fifteen would be safer. Then there could come a parting of the ways, and Mortimer might be reconciled to the upheaval that would follow. But it would not be.

And hadn't she said something now?

'Yes, Cook?'

'I was saying, this is Jane again, ma'am.'

'Yes. Jane. Ah yes, Jane.'

She must deal with the girl.

She found herself reaching for the embroidery on the

table beside her chair, the new bands for looping back the curtains in the library. Angrily she jerked away.

'Well – Well, Jane, do I find you in a better frame of mind today?'

The girl's face – really she was getting quite pretty, in a lumpish way – went a heavy sullen red.

'Yes, ma'am. I'm ever so sorry, ma'am.'

Perhaps it would all go smoothly. But she must not leave it here. The girl had been wrong. She truly had.

'Jane, I do not want to have to show severity to my servants. You must know that.'

'Oh yes, ma'am.'

A quick breath. One. And plunge again.

'But, Jane, I have to see that proper standards are maintained. It is my duty to do so. Just as it is your duty to do your work thoroughly and well. Do you understand that?'

In the girl's eyes there flared up what looked for a dreadful moment like the beginnings of another outburst, shouting that she had always done her work well, that she was being unfairly accused. But it was a moment only, and then the head drooped and the answer came quietly.

'Yes, ma'am.'

For one instant Mrs Johnson wondered whether she could count her task as done. But she knew that she could not. If only Cook had not been there. But, no, the girl had not been rebuked at all for the offence for which she had been brought up in the first place.

Another breath, another effort.

'Now, Jane, what Cook told me of your conduct on Thursday night was not at all what I like to hear. You are given time to go out every week. That is a privilege, Jane. And in return you owe a duty. That duty is not to be late back in. Ever.'

'But – '

Mercifully the sound had been so slight that she could with decency ignore it.

'No, ma'am. I'm very sorry, ma'am.'

Mrs Johnson felt a rush of relief. Earnestly she poured out the words she felt that she could say.

'What would happen if we were all late for those tasks to which we have been called, Jane? What would happen if the Master was late at his office in the City in the mornings? What – '

'But he – '

And, mercifully again, the interruption was checked, bitten back.

'What would happen, Jane, if I were not here at ten o'clock each morning to order the meals? The household would soon be at sixes-and-sevens, wouldn't it?'

'Yes, ma'am. Oh yes, ma'am.'

Perhaps the girl had been made to see how wrong she was.

'So you are repentant, Jane? Truly repentant?'

The eyes were downcast.

'Oh yes, ma'am. Truly.'

'Very well. We will say no more about it. But, remember, Jane, you cannot expect me always to be lenient. If Cook has occasion once again to tell me that you are disobedient or that you are not doing your duty as you should, then I shall know that you are a wicked girl at heart. And then, Jane, I shall have no hesitation in dismissing you. Is that understood?'

'Oh yes, ma'am, yes. Yes, I understand.'

Had the girl looked up with a glint of bitterness? At the very last moment? No, surely not. Surely not.

G

'Very well then, Jane, you may go back to your work.'

'Yes, ma'am. Thank you, ma'am. Thank you.'

And she curtsied properly and was gone.

'It's a bad look-out, lad,' Noll Sproggs said. 'A bad look-out.'

Val, once more reduced to standing a suppliant in front of the round table in the putter-up's little back parlour, wrestled with his mind to force himself into a more favourable notion of their prospects. But, for once, the reality was too obstinate for him.

'But yer can't fully blame Janey, Mr Sproggs,' he said dismally. 'She's been palled once, round behind that screen a-trying ter get a look at that door. If she's seen near it again, it's the sack fer 'er an' no mistake.'

The putter-up looked at him, cold gooseberry eyes unmoved.

'Then if she ain't no use ter you,' he said. 'No more you ain't no use ter me.'

He sighed. Heavily and puffily. Making a performance of it, a performance designed to cross the footlights.

'So I'll 'ave ter look elsewhere,' he said. 'See p'raps about makin' a nose out of a cove as goes in the 'ouse regular. Get the truth on it out of a gas-fitter or a bell-hanger. Or maybe the flue faker. After all, they got ter 'ave their chimneys swep', ain't they?'

He cocked an eye up at Val that was like a knife pointing towards his throat.

'But, Mr Sproggs, yer can't — Yer can't ditch me. Mr Sproggs, I done a lot fer yer on this bust. Wasn't I the one as put yer on ter it in the very start? Yer can't turn me off of it now. Yer can't.'

The white toad-face was as untouched as carved wax. The

hoarse voice whispered back the answer Val well knew that it would.

'I can, boy. I can. What's ter stop me?'

Val had nothing to offer. A great shelterless grey plain stretched out in front of him without the least break.

But the hoarse voice had something still to say.

'I gives yer a week, lad. Out o' the kindness o' me heart. One week. Get that girl o' yourn ter see that plate-closet door within the week, an' yer can stay on the bust. Otherwise . . . Well, otherwise I wouldn't come a-drinking in Newel Street no more, not if I was you.'

And Val was reduced to mere pleading.

'But it's 'ard on Janey, Mr Sproggs. Truly it is. The poor judy's been a-telling me half the arternoon. 'Er every minute in that 'ouse 'as ter be accounted fer, so ter speak. They knows where she ought ter be from first thing of a mornin' till last at night. Aye, an' all night too. If she were ter be caught a-wandering with a candle jus' now, it'd be up to the Mistress fer 'er quick as lightning. That Cook's told 'er so a-many times since she got off before.'

He knew that he was doing no more than talk, repeating at secondhand the tearful explanation Janey had given and given him under the full-blooming chestnut-trees of Kensington Gardens. But he had nothing to put in place of the toothless words that would stand any real chance of convincing the weasel-wary putter-up.

And Noll Sproggs showed not a jot of mercy more.

'She's got ter take the risk, lad, that's all. Tell 'er. Climbing Charlie ain't a-going in there not without 'e knows all about that plate-closet door. It ain't worth 'is while, an' I agree with 'im. So tell 'er ter creep it, an' creep it soon. If as 'ow yer wants ter drink in Newel Street.'

Val almost groaned aloud in manacled despair.

'I've told 'er, Mr Sproggs. I kep' on at 'er. On an' on at 'er. But the kid ain't like you an' me. She ain't been brought up ter thieve an' dodge. Why, if I was ter be in there – '

He broke off.

The idea that had jumped into his mind seemed at first appearance so ridiculous that he felt he should not even have thought it. Yet, wasn't it perhaps . . .

CHAPTER IX

ON THE MORNING of the following Monday, which was the tenth of June, Janey was waiting in the big kitchen at No 53, hovering not far from the area door under pretext of hanging some damp drying-up cloths above the quietly smouldering range. She was in a state of acute apprehension, fear and excitement snickering at her stomach. It was three minutes after ten o'clock.

The kitchen was cool and grey for all the sunshine just feeling its strength outside. The north-facing window, sunken in the area, seldom at any hour of the day or time of the year was crossed by sunlight and the bright unbroken blue sky that was alone just visible through it sent only the palest wash of light into the big room. The great kitchen-table, scrubbed daily till its pale brown boards, grooved and ridged with long hours of work, were now almost white, rested four-squarely on its sturdy legs, bare at this moment, awaiting the flurry of luncheon preparations to come. Under it the wide stone flags of the floor well still just wet from Janey's washing of them not long before. Across on the far side from the glinting black-leaded range the tall dresser stood with its array of white servants-use plates, its jugs and its dishes looking like so many patches of moonlight in the quiet summery duskiness. No one was about. The damped-down fire in the range shifted once, sending out a quiet grumble of complaint. The pendulum clock on the wall tocked softly.

Rat-tat-a-tat-tat.

The knocking, for all that Janey had been awaiting it, nerves stretched, made her jump in the air as if someone had poked a pin hard into her flesh. For several moments she stood shaking with the shock. Then she hurried over to the door.

When she turned the key in the lock and opened Val had his hand on the knocker again. Stepping back, he gave her a colossal cheerful wink.

'Val,' she said, in a thudding-heart excited whisper.

But he took no notice and instead spoke up in a voice that must have rung through the empty kitchen behind her.

'Good mornin', me dear. Any nice rabbit-skins for sale this bright blue mornin'?'

A smile, mischievous even, in response to his bravado, came up to her face. And, soon hardly able to suppress laughter, she went through the pantomime that had been agreed between them on the Friday before in a hurried 6.30 a.m. exchange out on the steps. Caught equally between the bubbling laughter and an inner pounding excitement that was more than half sheer fright, she left him at the door, went back into the kitchen, crossed its cool flagstones and went into the larder. There, tucked away out of sight, she had left a fine skin, which she had succeeded in pulling off complete. Sold to the regular rabbit-skin man on his customary Friday call it would have earned her a useful sixpence to add to the small savings in the little wash-leather purse deep at the bottom of her box. But she sacrificed that gladly.

She picked up the skin, feeling it as having gone a little hard during its wait in hiding. Then she stood where she was, as she had agreed with Val, and began counting. Val had asked her for three minutes, 'till you count two hundred, slow.' It ought, they had decided, to be long

enough for him to dart on tip-toe across the kitchen and
on to the foot of the backstairs, knowing from her directions just where he had to go. Then up the stairs, fast as he
could but keeping well to the edge for quietness, and open
the first green-baize door he came to. One quick peep,
in case by some unlikely chance there was someone about in
the hall, and then over to the breakfast-room, once more
knowing exactly where to go. He would not need as much
as half a minute behind the screen looking at that door, he
had told her. Half a minute to do what Climbing Charlie
had asked, 'study it like it was the will of a old gentleman
a-leaving you his fortun' ', and then he would know everything the cracksman might inquire about it. Half a minute
on his own behind the worked-leather screen. And this
morning there would be no Mr Burch coming unexpectedly
out of the closet, not when he was, as she had made sure
earlier, safely out on the morning walk he almost always
took to pass the time of day with the butler along at
No 47 during this their quiet hour. Half a minute for Val
and then back the way he had come, and, if she timed it
right, there he would be out in the area again just as she
came up with the rabbit skin.

Twelve, thirteen, fourteen . . . Slowly she counted, giving
a little stroke to the furry pelt at each number. Sixteen,
seventeen —

'And who are you? And what are you doing in my
kitchen?'

Even through the heavy closed door of the larder she
heard it. Mrs Vickers' voice. Mrs Vickers' voice raised in
loud indignation. And right outside. Right outside, where
at ten o'clock in the morning, her time for discussing with
the Mistress the day's meals regular as clockwork, she should
not possibly be.

'It's – Sure, I'm just a rabbit-skin man, missus.'

Val. Sounding more Irish than usual, putting it on for all he was worth. But Janey, who had listened to that voice with such an intensity of love, could tell that under the brave assurance he was in a panic of fear.

'Rabbit skins. Rabbit skins. I'll give you rabbit skins. How does buying a rabbit skin bring you right into my kitchen, I'd like to know.'

Janey clutched so hard at the stiff skin in her hands that her nails almost dug through it.

'It was . . .' came Val's voice, fumbling more now. 'It was – The kitchen-maid told me she'd a skin to sell, missus.'

'Well, she's a slut if there ever was. Going to give you a cup of tea, I dare say. Thinks when my back's turned she can play fast and loose with the Mistress's provisions.'

'Ah, no, missus, no. 'Twasn't like that at all, at all. I swear to God it wasn't. She just went to the larder to fetch a skin as she told me she'd got.'

'Oh, she did, did she? Well, I'll give her larder. Going off and leaving the area door wide open like that. I just happen to come down to see how much cold beef we got over, because the Mistress takes it into her head . . . And what do I find? Janey! Janey, where are you?'

And Janey, still digging with her work-broken nails into the rabbit skin, realized that no longer was the overheard scene outside an event taking place without her being in any way able to influence it, passionately though the outcome concerned her. Now the finger was pointing directly at her.

'Janey!'

She forced herself to the door, wrenched at the knob, and, her mind whirling, presented herself in front of Mrs Vickers.

'Now, then, what's all this about letting this man in here?'

Janey swallowed and thanked heaven for the preparations they made over their story.

'Please, Mrs Vickers, it's the rabbit-skin man. I been to fetch a skin I got fer 'im.'

'Oh, you have, have you? And don't you know better than to leave the door open so's any sort of rapscallion can make his way in? Really, the girls I'm expected to get along with under me. It's no wonder things never go right. If they're not lazy, they're stupid. And if they're not stupid, they're downright sly.'

'Yes, Mrs Vickers.'

'And don't you "Yes, Mr Vickers" me.' She whipped suddenly round to Val who had been glancing across to the distant area door, measuring his distance. 'And don't you think I've forgotten you either, my man. What were you doing right across here, for one thing? Not one word of explanation have I had for that.'

'No, missus, no,' Val muttered, plainly searching for some shred of excuse.

'Well, speak up, speak up. Or do I have to send the girl for the policeman?'

And then she took a pouncing step nearer him.

'You're not the regular rabbit-skin man either,' she proclaimed. 'Friday's his day. Friday. And here's it's Monday. What are you, I should like to know!'

This is it, Janey thought. It's come to it now. He's caught. We're both caught.

She felt numb through and through, incapable of speech, incapable of action, incapable of thought.

But Val was not as dumbstruck, by any means. Mrs Vickers's words had apparently given him a clue. A wide, soft, wheedling smile spread across his face.

'Ah, sure, you've the right on it there, missus,' he said,
Irish as Killarney. 'Sure, an' I knows well the other feller
comes of a Friday. An' it's thinkin' to meself I am "What
if I was to come on a Monday, and maybe like get there
before him".'

'Disgraceful,' Mrs Vickers exploded. 'Disgraceful. You've
no business to be doing an honest man out of his living like
that. No business at all.'

Janey held her breath in sheer suspense. Val was skilfully
edging Mrs Vickers away from the danger area, bringing a
cunning she had hitherto only had glimpses of to the repair
of the gaping damage that chance had torn in their plan.

Then step by step Val went on with his work, with many
an Irish compliment to Mrs Vickers's 'divilish sharp eye,'
with a cautious half-pace there and a sideways shuffle here,
with a profuse tumbling-out all the while of 'Good day,
missus' and 'Thank you indeed, missus'.

He reached the door. Mrs Vickers's denunciations of his
commercial wickedness rose to a peak. He backed along to
the stone steps leading up to pavement level. He started
to climb, turned still to cast out dollops of Irish reassurance.
Mrs Vickers, her arms akimbo, raised up her head the
better to lambaste him. And then he was at the top of the
steps, and in a wink he was away, feet running hard till
the corner was reached.

So dash and skill in the heat and smoke of battle can
enable half-a-dozen hussars to outmanœuvre a whole
squadron of dragoons.

But if Val escaped, Janey paid for it. The skirmish seemed
to have sharpened to an altogether new pitch Mrs Vickers's
ill will, sharp enough in any case ever since she had

managed to scrape her way out of trouble up before the Mistress.

For the fourth or fifth time since the morning incident she was undergoing a verbal thrashing at the Cook's hands as she scurried in and out of the servants' hall clearing away the supper dishes.

'It's all very well for you, my girl,' the nail-hammering voice went on. 'It's all very well for you. You haven't got a whole kitchen on your shoulders. You haven't got six courses to send up of a night and every one of 'em to be perfect. It's a fine life for the likes of you.'

'Fine life,' Janey let herself murmur, carrying out a fat pile of dirty plates. 'It's miserable, miserable.'

'What was that?'

Her tormentor came out into the kitchen after her.

'What did I hear you say?'

Janey longed to turn and answer that if Mrs Vickers had heard she had no need to ask what had been said. But she fought with herself and ran into the scullery in silence. A moment later the Cook's irate form was blocking the door behind her.

'I won't have muttering in my kitchen, d'you hear? I won't have it. Speak up now, speak up.'

Janey then was unable to hold herself in any longer. She let the pile of plates crash down on the wooden draining-board and hurled herself round.

'I said my life's a misery,' she flung out.

'And whose fault is that, I should like to know,' Mrs Vickers came swinging back, seeming the more delighted to have opposition. 'Whose fault is that? It's your own, my girl. Yours and nobody else's. You've got no one but yourself to blame if you're always getting into hot water. You do things the way they ought to be done, and I promise you you'll not find yourself at the sharp end of my tongue.'

'Even when I do do things right, you never believe me,' Janey retorted.

'Oh, I don't, don't I? And I'll tell you why not. It's because you don't do things right, my lass. You don't do a single thing right. You're all alike you girls today : think wishing's doing, got your minds always on something else than the work you ought to be at. That's your trouble. Well, the sooner you make a change the better for you. You can't wish away that rabbit-skin man this morning, no more than you can wish away the dirt on a floor you haven't properly scrubbed.'

'I only left him for a moment,' Janey answered, almost too weary of her lie to utter it with proper conviction. 'I wasn't ter know he'd come right into the kitchen.'

'And you wasn't to know he wouldn't,' Mrs Vickers answered with clanging delight, advancing into the suds-smelling little room like a turkey-cock. 'And that I won't have, d'you hear? Letting riff-raff like that into my kitchen. And the Master taking on so about burglars.'

And then, the chance words that had come into her head in the rattle and spate of her denunciation leading her on with inevitable logic, she brought forth a threat which at the outset must have been completely outside her intentions.

'Yes, and you'll have to go up to him, you know. You'll have to see the Master. You can't get away from that.'

Janey felt the unexpected edict as a smack across her cheek.

A pit opened before her and she tumbled head-over-heels into it, falling through and through the blackness. She had thought that the week before she had bent and beseeched her way out of trouble. She had thought she had kept her little secure niche in the house then. She had thought that, by taming herself beyond what she had believed she could endure, she had above all kept her place in Val's heart. And now, with a suddenness that was totally inexplicable, everything was being taken away from her.

She saw it all. Up before the Master, a figure ten and twenty times more terrible than the Mistress. Instant dismissal. Not a word of a character. Thrown out. Lost in the wide world. And cast equally and by the same stroke out of Val's love. No use to him, thrown away, a rag.

Not knowing even that she was doing it, she lifted up her head in dog-like lamentation.

'Oh, it's no use your howling,' she heard Mrs Vickers's voice, darting and pricking like a hornet round her ears. 'It's no use your howling. My mind's made up. It's to the Master for you. You'd have been up to him tonight, only he's out at the opera and dinner first at his Club. Oh yes, you would. But it's straight away in the morning instead, I promise you that. Soon as he's ready to see you.'

Janey howled and howled. Her miseries presented themselves to her now as going on and on till the end of the world. And to lament to the heavens was all she could do in face of the prospect.

And then into the doorway behind Mrs Vickers there came another figure. Tall, a pillar, grave. Mr Burch.

'Now, what is all this?' he asked, his voice firm and clear. 'You've no business to be making a noise like that, my girl. Stop it at once.'

Janey stopped. And, given again the capability of speech, she answered the butler's question.

'Oh, Mr Burch. Mr Burch, it's that she says I've got to go and see the Master. An' he'll turn me away. I know he will. He can't do nothing else, being so particular over locks an' all.'

'Locks?' said Mr Burch sharply.

He turned to Mrs Vickers.

'Has this girl been leaving doors unlocked?'

'Worse,' Mrs Vickers replied in triumph. 'Worse, by far. She's been letting all sorts come right into my kitchen.'

'Is that the rabbit-skin man you were mentioning at dinner-time?' Mr Burch asked.

'Yes, it is,' said Mrs Vickers. 'Allowing a fellow of that sort to come planting his dirty boots all over my kitchen floor.'

Mr Burch coughed.

'Well, Mrs Vickers,' he answered, 'it may not be altogether my place to say this, but I think we have heard enough about that business. Janey may have been wrong to turn her back on the fellow, but I can't say I've ever had anything to complain of about her otherwise, which is more than I can say for most of the kitchen-maids I've known. But if the Master did get to hear that a stranger had set foot inside the house Janey would get turned away, and you know it. So I think the less said on that score the better.'

Mrs Vickers bridled.

'Well, I'm sure I never wished the girl harm,' she said.

Janey saw the butler's gaze turn towards her.

'Then you had better tell Mrs Vickers for one last time that you're truly sorry about this morning,' he said. 'And then we'll hear no more about it.'

Janey felt the stars in their courses swing to new, altogether unheard-of places. To be saved. Saved when she had felt herself lost for ever. Saved so unexpectedly. And saved, above all, by Mr Burch, that distant, always unchangeably correct figure, as far from her in many ways as the Master and Mistress themselves. To have him reach down, step out of his unvarying path and pick her up. It was a miracle. It was the world turned an altogether new way.

Mr Burch.

Her heart welling with gratitude, she stumbled out an apology to Mrs Vickers. The last words on the subject. The bringing to an end of what had a few moments earlier seemed to be an on-and-on downwards-going plunge. And now it was over.

She swayed in incredulity.

Mr Burch. Mr Burch. What he had done for her. What wouldn't she do for him, from now on and for ever.

So first thing next morning Val, creeping up to the gate of No 53 more cautiously than ever but determined to find out whether his upset plan of the day before had or had not wrecked their whole venture, received, when he hissed a greeting to Janey, an altogether different reception from anything he had imagined.

'Hsst. Janey. Janey, is everything all right?'

He saw her jump, startled. Then she turned to him. But at once she checked, and for a moment it looked as if she was going to go back to the brass door-handle she had been busy rubbing. But she faced him steadily at last.

'Go away,' she said.

He darted a probing glance at the tall white façade of the house. Was there a detective-officer there, waiting for him?

All seemed well.

'Janey, is it safe?' he asked urgently.

'It's safe enough, but go away.'

He felt a small spurt of anger. What was she at?

'Janey, did they twig? Did they ask yer questions?'

The fierceness of his tone evidently compelled her to answer.

'No. No, they didn't. Mrs Vickers went on at me, but . . .'

'But what? What is it, Janey?'

She came down two or three steps towards him. Her face was tight-drawn and white in the early morning sunshine.

'Val,' she said, 'I don't know which way to turn. Val, I loves yer. But – But, Mr Burch.'

'Old fool. What about him?'

'Val, yesterday she was going ter send me up ter the Master. Mrs Vickers. It'd 'ave meant the sack, Val. I'd 'ave been out on the street. I don't know what I should 'ave done. I've nowhere ter go. I'd of died, Val. There wouldn't 'ave been nothing else ter do. But then Mr Burch, 'e stepped in an' saved me. He good as told 'er she were a interfering cow, Val. Val, 'e saved me.'

He frowned, feeling cheated of something though he did not quite know what.

'Well,' he said, ' 'e saved yer.'

She shook her head slowly in wonder.

'I didn't know 'e 'ad that side to 'im,' she said. 'Never in all the time I been 'ere. It only shows as 'ow folk ain't a-always what we thinks. It do truly.'

She stood pondering, seeing new things.

Val felt a surge of impatience, of dislike of the whole situation.

'Ach, the feller happened by chance ter be feeling good,' he said. 'An' he put in a word fer yer. That's the whole on it.'

'No, Val, no. The more I thinks, the more I sees.

There's more to Mr Burch than "Do yer duty". There is, Val, there is.'

She straightened her back in the shapeless print frock he had grown to know so well.

'An', Val,' she said. 'That's why I don't want no more ter do with it.'

'With it? With what?'

He shot the questions out like a swift rattle of muskets. But only because underneath he knew well what the answers were.

'With you breakin' in 'ere of a night, Val,' she replied simply. 'I wouldn't want Mr Burch done no 'arm. Not now.'

'But it ain't him we'd be doing any 'arm,' he argued fiercely back. 'It's not 'is plate we're a-going ter lay our 'ands on.'

For a moment he thought he might have won. But Janey was only thinking out her answer.

'It may not be 'is plate,' she said at last. 'But, Val, 'e polishes it as if it were. I seen 'im, Val, when 'e brings pieces down ter the kitchen sometimes of an arternoon. I know it. It'd fair break 'is 'eart to 'ave them things gone.'

'There'd be others got fer 'im soon enough,' he answered with savagery. 'Folk like the folk in there just buys new again when their crib's cracked.'

Janey was hesitating once more before replying. She must be seeing the truth of what he had said. She must.

He plunged here and there in his mind for further arguments of the same sort. But he was too late.

'No, Val,' she said. 'No. I know as 'ow Mr Burch would never feel the same. Not when 'e's polished an' petted those

H

things for years, the way I know 'e 'as.'

Once more she lifted her face to him and looked at him with defiance.

'No, Val, no,' she said. 'I won't do it. I won't 'elp yer no more, Val, an' that's an end on it.'

He felt the anger rise. He felt it come scorching and blazing up him.

And she must have seen it too, because as plainly he saw rage leap up in her.

'No,' she said, her voice clear and ringing, careless of what might be heard or who might hear it. 'No, I won't do it. Not never. An' yer can tell that to yer thievin' friends.'

For a single black instant he was tempted to leap at once over the ironwork gate, seize her and fling her to the ground.

But then the thought of all that the house behind her meant to him came rolling up like a raincloud to drench a burning landscape. And he forced the breath from his body in a long whistling hiss.

'Janey,' he said. 'Janey. If that's the way yer feels, it's the way yer feels. But it's not to come between the two on us, Janey. We're more to each other than that, Janey mine.'

And at the words her tears flowed.

He let them come for only half a minute, desperately conscious of all the noise they both had been making and of the danger it brought. Then in a few hurried whisperings he comforted her and warned her and promised to see her in the usual way on Thursday and left.

But he left with a leaden heart.

CHAPTER X

So IN THE OPENING stages of a campaign, when the attacking troops are still moving forward in good order, still adhering to the paper-plans drawn up by the General's staff long before the first order to advance was ever given, then at certain points they begin to encounter the defending outworks and then unknown strengths, long inbuilt though perhaps concealed by slow growths of time, may unexpectedly manifest themselves. There enter at this point into the pattern of the battle those first quirks and circumstances of chance that touch and upset even the best-laid plans. And it is now that the field-officers are put to the test. It is the manner in which they meet the unexpected that often dictates the whole outcome of the affair ahead.

It had been, for instance, the sole initiative of Climbing Charlie that brought him on Wednesday, the twelfth of June, one day before Noll Sproggs's time-limit to Val was due to expire, to the quiet street not ten minutes' walk from Northbourne Park Villas where Val himself had tried to persuade Janey for the last time to tell him about the door of the plate-closet and where she had given him an answer he had not at all expected.

Charlie, lording it in the bar of the gin-shop in Newel Street two nights earlier waiting for the putter-up to return from some mysterious errand and feeling all a-glow with life, had seen the lad Val come in. He had looked so hang-dog that he had laughed out loud at the sight. He had chaffed him a bit too, more than a bit even. And then the story had come out. The lad's notion of playing the rabbit-skin man, the unexpected arrival in the kitchen of the cook at the place, the lad's ridiculous flight. ' 'Cor,' Charlie had said, tears of laughter in his eyes. ' 'Cor, I wouldn't 'alf 'ave liked to 'ave seen 'er, seen that old Cookie a-chasing you out of 'er kitchen.' And then the lad had angrily asked whether he realized that this meant the whole bust was off. And in a second he had flared back with a promise to set up the whole thing all on his own and with never a word to old Noll Sproggs. ' 'Ere,' he had laughed, 'I'll 'ave to prig that old Cookie's savings one day, I'll 'ave to, that's what.' And that had led him, dressed to the nines in his suit of brown Prince-of-Wales check, his brown curly-brimmed bowler jauntily set, to a cleverly contrived meeting with the lady's-maid at No 53, the lad at least having had the savvy to know when her day out was, and on to this moment here in the street not far from the house, with a bagful of things he had learnt from her already and, if he knew anything, within an inch of hearing all about that plate-closet.

Just one step further into her mind, one little risky step, and he would have her. The music-hall they had just come from had done most of the work for him. She had begun by pretending not to hear the jokes in the songs that went a bit near the knuckle, then she had pretended not to understand when he had winked at her to point them, but soon she had smiled and at last she had laughed. So he had got himself nicely behind the frozen-faced outside already. All he needed now was to make her feel that he was quite at home there, and she would be in such a state that he could ask her anything.

Then, what a piece of luck, he spied a couple of cats going at it like one o'clock just on the far pavement.

' 'Ere,' he said, swinging his arm round so that Rosa, hanging on to it, was turned directly to face the hot cats. ' 'Ere, someone's going ter 'ave ter explain a basketful o' kittens a couple o' months from now.'

She blushed. But she giggled too, as he knew she would.

'Oh, Mr Charlie,' she said, 'you are a one. The things you say . . .'

'Bit too much like a clergyman, am I?' he quipped.

Her trill of laughter – silly bitch – rang out in the dusky street.

'Oh, Mr Charlie, why I ever allowed you to walk home with me when you're no more than a chance acquaintance I don't know.'

'It's 'cos we get on so well,' he said, leaning towards her and encountering a strong whiff of flowery scent which, he bet himself a shilling, was pinched from the Mistress. 'Funny 'ow we should get on really, considerin' the accidental way o' the meeting.'

'Yes. Oh yes.'

She slowed her pace yet more, and actually turned and looked up at him, her papery face moony as a cow's.

'Perhaps it's because the meeting was Intended,' she breathed.

For an instant he thought she was on to him. Then he realized what she had meant. Well, at least it showed he was there, home and dry in her mind.

Now for it.

' 'Ere,' he said, contriving to sound suddenly over-whelmed. ' 'Ere, give us a kiss.'

She drew herself up a little and came to a full halt.

'What,' she said, 'right here by the street-lamp? I don't know what you think I am.'

'You're a lovely woman, that's what,' Charlie at once

replied, unchecked by the display of coyness.

He transferred the arm to which she had been clinging to a position round her waist, feeling with his fingertips the whalebones of the corset under the white silk of her elaborate dress no doubt inherited from her Mistress.

She tossed her head at his compliment.

'Well, I dare say I do contrive to make the best of myself,' she admitted.

'You want ter let me make the best o' you, me dear,' Charlie said.

He glanced quickly along the street and spotted the opening to a narrow high-walled alley running between the gardens of two of the big houses. It looked more than promising.

'Listen,' he added quickly. 'Let's take a stroll along that passageway. Bit o' dark there.'

'Certainly not.'

Charlie was unabashed. They always liked to put up a show, this sort. But he'd end up by getting her a yard or two along that alleyway. And there he'd kiss her. All in the cause of duty. And then she'd tell him anything, anything at all he wanted. That he knew.

'Ah, come on,' he said to her, cheerfully and easily. 'Lovely creature like you. Why shouldn't you?'

'Because I knows how to keep myself to myself, and always have done,' she answered haughtily.

Inwardly Charlie grinned. The haughtier they got, the harder they fell.

But suddenly he felt her stiffen inside his encircling arm.

'And besides,' she said, with a new scratchier note. 'Besides, there's another reason.'

'Another reason? What's that then?'

He kept his head close to hers and his voice down to a murmur.

'It's not a what. It's a who.'

'A who?' He allowed himself to move away a little and pretended to perk himself up. 'I got a rival then?' he asked. 'Where is he? Just show him ter me. Just let me see the feller.'

'All right then,' she answered quite unexpectedly, slipping out of his arm and giving herself a little shake. 'Look down at the far end of the street there.'

Charlie looked, more than a little puzzled at the turn events were taking. And he saw on the far side, shadowy but unmistakable in the light of the lamp at the corner, the tall helmeted silhouette of a policeman.

He choked.

'A bluebottle. A bloody bluebottle.'

'You'll mind your language,' Rosa rebuked him sharply, making him suddenly realize how far the situation was slipping from his grasp. 'Mind your language. Remember, you're out with a lady.'

And then she added, almost too quietly to be heard, four quick words, 'Not that he did.'

'Not that he – You mean you been out with 'im. You been going with a bluebottle?'

'Going, indeed,' Rosa said. 'I'll have you to know I'm careful whom I allow to become too closely acquainted with me.'

'All right then,' Charlie asked, 'what about him?'

Rosa lifted her well-bonneted hair-piled head into the air.

'He happened to step up one evening,' she said, 'just as I was a-making my way home. He happened to pass a remark, and we happened to talk.'

'What then?' Charlie asked.

'He made a certain suggestion,' Rosa answered distantly.

'Just like the boys in blue,' Charlie put in quickly, seeing a chance to re-establish his position. 'And what next?'

'I told him what I thought of him. Of course.'

'Of course,' he agreed. 'And then?'

'Then he had the impertinence to make a number of remarks.'

'Such as?'

'I won't stoop to repeat them.'

He waited in silence. If he knew anything, he would hear just what those remarks had been in less than two seconds.

'Well, what they amounted to was the suggestion – I don't know how he dared – that I wouldn't be able to get myself a gentleman friend not even if I . . .'

She tailed off.

'Not even?' Charlie prompted.

'Not even if I was willing to do a certain thing.'

She turned and looked across the street. The two cats were still there. She looked hastily away again.

'What an idea,' Charlie said with a great show of indignation. 'What an idea. Trust the Regiment o' Blues.'

'And that,' Rosa said, turning to him fully once again, 'is why it's a fine piece of luck for me to be walking this way in the company of a gentleman like you.'

'Like me?'

'The very respectable and well-dressed manager of a betting-office, if I may make so bold.'

Charlie saw now fully what she wanted. To parade her new acquaintance in front of the one who had been so scornful of her.

He swallowed.

'Yes,' he said. 'But — But a peeler.'

'Common as dirt,' Rosa snapped.

'I know. I know. But . . .'

'So,' Rosa went on, all determination now, every papery inch of her. 'If you please, we'll step along a little lively.'

'No.'

It was all he could think of to say.

'No? What do you mean "No"?'

'Let's — Let's go along the passageway there.'

'Certainly not.'

But then Rosa smiled with terrible archness.

'Or not until after we've gone a-walking right past Policeman Watson, No 126,' she said.

Charlie looked across the road at the advancing bluebottle. He was already much nearer. And the pair of them were standing just where the lamplight fell on their side. If he was to cut and run he would draw all the attention in the world to himself.

He gulped.

'All right,' he said, feeling then the sweat spring up and as well a thudding of excitement that was both familiar and intoxicating. 'All right, let's walk.'

And walk they did, Charlie offering Rosa his arm again and she prinking along beside him with a carriage that would have done credit to any actress at Drury Lane.

But when they at last drew level with Policeman Watson, No 126 — happily exactly in the darkness between two lamps — what Rosa did was worse than Charlie's worst forebodings.

She looked full across the street and spoke in a voice that would have been audible even to the back row of the gods at the music-hall.

'Good night, Mr Policeman.'

It was too much for Charlie. He froze in horror as the heavily perambulating Policeman Watson slowly turned and looked into the darkness straight at the voice that had hailed him.

But mercifully he turned away, and in the dark as his steps slowly receded, Charlie tried to produce his carefree smile again.

But it was too late. Rosa had dropped his arm and was peering hard into his face.

'Why,' she said, 'you were ashamed to look that fellow in the eye. Yes, you were. I thought there was something funny about you when he first came along, and I see it all now. You're not the betting-office manager you said. You're not. You're nothing but a criminal.'

'No, no, I'm not,' Charlie replied ineffectually.

'Oh yes, you are. You're what the Master calls a member of the dangerous classes. And now I see why you were so keen to take a lady to the music-hall and offer her refreshment afterwards. You wanted to find out all about our place. You're nothing but a cracksman intent on burgling us all. Nothing but a cracksman.'

And then, as she evidently came to a full realization of just how completely she had been deceived, her last shreds of dignity went whistling away.

'You beast,' she hissed out. 'You filthy beast.'

And her fingernails, not blunted and cracked like most servants' but finely filed and tiger-sharp, rose to his face.

An hour later Charlie entered the Newel Street gin-shop with all his jauntiness restored, though not without a dark-red tell-tale scratch mark all the way down his left cheek. As he came in he saw Noll Sproggs himself

standing behind the bar, with an unmistakable air of
sentry-go. And in a second the squat putter-up had ducked
through under the bar and was coming towards him.
And his greenish eyes were unexpectedly filled with
stone-hard anger.

'Out,' he said, thrusting his white face forward. 'Out, an'
quick.'

' 'Ere, what is all – '

'You get out an' don't yer come near this place till
a month's gone, every day on it.'

Charlie bristled.

'I got a right – '

'Just yer listen ter me,' the putter-up said, his hoarse
voice full of sharp intent. 'Yer know Old Henry, the
crow, best watcher and waiter in all London? He 'appened
ter be in 'ere last night an' heard you an' that lad a-making
your plan. Had a word with me, he did. I've 'eard all
about you and that crusher not two hour back. Paradin'
yerself in front o' him. He's the cove on the beat there, yer
know. Northbourne Park Villas is on 'is walk. An' 'e was
on ter yer. Old Henry saw him arter, an' 'e could tell. You
was palled right enough, an' I don't want ter see yer 'ere
again. That's the flat on it.'

Charlie had fought for a little during this fiercely
whispered outburst to keep his grin on his face. But
before very long he let it fade. There was only one course
open to him now.

Noll Sproggs was never going to let his place be coupled
with any cove the peelers had their eye on, no matter who.

He did not attempt any word of parting, but simply
turned on his heel and sloped off out. There was the
rookery at St Giles, and he would be better lying low there
for a spell if things were the way old Sproggsie had said.

The lower he kept his head and the longer he kept it low from now on, the better for his health.

In the parlour behind the bar, the light of the solitary oil-lamp sending flickering orangey reflections off the gleaming wood of the surrounding cupboards, Val sat on a hard chair in one corner, frozen in gloom. Up at the round table, on a chair placed confidentially close to the putter-up's own empty one, sat Old Henry, the crow, not far from being a warder.

Ever since Val had arrived, expecting Charlie to come cheerfully breezing in with the news that he himself had seen the door of the plate-closet at No 53 and that there was now no obstacle to the bust, he had been kept prisoner in the parlour. The ever-suspicious Noll Sproggs was not going to risk him seeing Charlie first and perhaps softening the tongue-lashing warning-off he intended to give out.

So there in the corner Val sat. And up at the table sat Old Henry, saying never a word but every now and again letting a little dark furtive grin cross his old chops. A little dark furtive fellow altogether was Old Henry, in his rusty black coat pulled close about him despite the warmth of the evening, with his rusty black broken-crowned stovepipe hat jammed hard on to a pair of sticking-out ears plainly grimed with layered dirt even in the chancy lamplight.

Val had not been surprised at the look of him when they had met, not after hearing Noll Sproggs call him 'the best crow in London, the very best.' His life, it seemed, was dedicated to watching, to watching houses, to watching policemen, to watching his fellow members of the criminal fraternity, and, at its highest moments, to watching while a bust was in progress at some big toffken or richly-packed warehouse. Then he kept look-out, snarlingly suspicious of every sound and movement, ready at the least hint of police activity to make his warning signal for the cracksmen inside either to lie low or make their escape. Light appearing in an unexpected window, an unheralded visitor, any sign of a domestic upset that might alter a relied-upon routine, and Old Henry would send a dog's bark or cat's howl out into the night for the gang inside to hear.

A life devoted to the watching task had made him, Val had already discovered, ready to see the worst in anything and anybody always. Long hours of lurking in the dark, waiting for something to go wrong, had convinced him that in this world things are made to go wrong.

So now he sat, that dark gloating grin appearing every few minutes on his lean grey-stubbled jaws, as he thought no doubt that once again his view of the world had proved only too right. The give-away encounter between a known cracksman keeping close company with a maid-servant and the very policeman of all the men in the force who would know just where she lived was, true enough, a bad strike against the whole plan. But sitting there in the little parlour, silent and inwardly seething, Val wished and wished again that the old crow did not have to look so pleased about it.

At last the putter-up came in from the bar.

'Seen 'im,' he commented tersely. 'Gone.'

Val felt himself impelled to speak, though he knew that any word of his was more likely to bring down the putter-up's anger on his head.

'Mr Sproggs,' he said, 'ain't there no chance of it now? I been thinking, Mr Sproggs. Maybe it don't need anyone ter climb in. Ain't there places broke into with twirls? I could get a wax take o' the key to that front door from my Janey. I'm certain o' that.'

It was something he was far from sure of in view of the words he had heard from Janey out on the steps the last time he had seen her, 'I won't do it, not never, an' yer can tell that to yer thievin' friends,' but he saw no other way to keep the affair going. And this chance of a lifetime must not be let just die away.

Noll Sproggs went to his chair at the round table and put fresh gin from the little squat black bottle into his glass and Old Henry's. He said not a word.

Val swallowed.

'Wouldn't that do it, Mr Sproggs? A wax take, make a set o' twirls, an' me an' a feller as knew about crackin' a peter go in just afore the front door's bolted of a night an' hide somewhere till all's quiet. Wouldn't that do it?'

Again Noll Sproggs was silent. But after a little Old Henry allowed himself to speak.

'Go in there?' he said scathingly. 'Go in there? With detective officers a-sprouting like laurel bushes all over the garden. Yer must be a glock, if yer thinks any o' that's still in the wind.'

Unexpectedly this stream of vituperation caused Noll Sproggs to open his mouth.

'Yes,' he said. 'Yes, there'll be detective officers there right enough. But how long'll they stay? How long'll they stay?'

' 'Ow long?' Old Henry asked, as if he were weighing the likelihood of it being fifty years or a whole century.

'Maybe a month,' the putter-up answered his own question. 'Maybe even a bit longer. But then they'll go.'

'They'll not be gone inside o' five week,' Old Henry declared with a shake of his head.

'All right then,' Noll Sproggs retorted, turning to the old crow with a spark of anger. 'All right, six week. I don't care. Not when I got the 'vantage I 'ave now.'

' 'Vantage? What 'vantage?' Val could not restrain himself from asking, though he well knew that the less he drew attention to himself the better.

'The 'vantage o' that peeler,' Noll Sproggs replied, addressing himself so much to Old Henry that it might have appeared that he had put Val out of his mind altogether. 'Don't yer see it? It's not that the feller spotted Charlie, though that's bad as can be, I grant. But it's what we knows on 'im now.'

'We knows he's the feller on the beat for Northbourne Park Villas,' Old Henry said lugubriously.

'Pah,' Noll Sproggs answered. 'You overheard that Rosa say it herself of him. Don't yer see? That peeler's a man fer a girl an' a dark corner, chary though he may be o' showing it. But he is so, an' we knows it. An' that's worth its weight in gold.'

The dismal old crow drew in a long sucking whistling breath.

'Yerss,' he conceded. 'Yerss, you've the right on it, Mr Sproggs. It's strong. It's strong. There's nothing like a policeman what's a prey to lust.'

CHAPTER XI

IT WAS A LONG time however before Noll Sproggs made any outward move in his campaign against the house at No 53 Northbourne Park Villas. He even told Val to let Janey know the next day after Climbing Charlie's disaster when he saw her in Kensington Gardens that he would not be able to meet her there for all the coming month. 'Tell 'er as 'ow yer got work pickin' fruit down in Kent, lad.' And he made this ban good by sending Val down to a retired acquaintance by whom he was owed a favour to spend the four weeks in the fruit gardens, despite Val's tentative protest that this would deprive him of the company of his Eileen.

But the putter-up was not completely idle during this prudent absence of activity, as Val discovered when he got back to London. He had walked up from Kent along the dusty roads all one blazingly hot July day and had thankfully come in at last to the drink-odorous coolness of the gin-shop in Newel Street.

'Just in time, lad,' Noll Sproggs said to him across the metal-topped bar, his hoarse voice hardly audible. 'Just in time. Yer can come along o' me termorrer ter the Euston Station. There'll be somebody there as'd like to 'ave a look at you, I dare say. Be 'ere at eight in the evenin'. Eight sharp.'

And not a word more would he utter.

Nor did he say much more when next evening, the evening of July the tenth, Val, fresh from the arms of his restored Eileen, presented himself at the gin-shop. In almost complete silence the two of them travelled by omnibus to Euston, and even there the putter-up told Val only that they were to meet a train from Manchester and that on it there would be a cracksman from that northern city whom he had used on one occasion before and who was safely unknown to the London police. The Manchester Man, Noll Sproggs called him.

And there was something about his manner in referring to him, an even more than usual reluctance to give anything away, that made Val at once a little uneasy, though he would have found it hard to say why.

He stood watching the long minute hand of the great station clock jerk its way throb by throb towards the time the train was due. In front of him well-wrapped night-travellers hurried her and there, followed by solidly-capped porters laden with valises, hat-boxes and hampers. Every now and again a band of new arrivals would come surging out of one of the platform gates past the blue-uniformed, red-striped, capped ticket-collectors, peering this way and that in the steamy atmosphere to get their bearings. Everywhere there was an air of excitement. But Val knew that it was not this that was affecting him.

And then at last the long clock hand jerked on to the hour exactly. Noll Sproggs nudged him.

'The Mary Blane just a-coming in,' he said.

'Right you are,' Val answered, licking his lips quickly and dartingly as he saw along the silver-glinting rails the black round steam-plumed front of the locomotive of the Manchester express.

'Watch out fer a tall feller as they comes off. Tall, an' with a 'eavy pair o' black moustaches.'

The description was clear enough. But Val felt somehow that it was not the way in which Noll Sproggs actually

I

thought about 'the Manchester Man.' He watched as the great train hissed and puffed its way to rest on the far side of the iron railings of the barrier. It came to a final squealing halt a yard or so clear of the giant buffers and doors opened briskly all along the line of carriages. Porters hurried up with their trolleys. A few passengers began to step down. From the third-class, servants leapt out and hurried to the first to be ready to receive their masters.

Then, half a head taller than any of the first-comers, Val saw a man, heavy-browed under a pulled-down sealskin cap, wearing a great rough coat and marked out by a fine pair of heavy black drooping moustaches.

He touched the putter-up's elbow and pointed, though he had no doubt that the near-giant thrusting his way through the other passengers was the man they had come to meet.

'Yes, lad. That's 'im.'

The putter-up seemed displeased even to have had to say this much, and they waited in an unhappy silence until the towering figure on the far side reached the barrier, surrendered his ticket – he did this as if the act was blackly objectionable to him – and passed through the gate.

Then the putter-up stepped forward.

'Mr Outhwaite,' he said, with an obsequiousness of manner that came to Val as completely unusual. 'Pleased that you came, most pleased.'

'Mr Sproggs,' the Manchester Man answered curtly as could be.

The putter-up actually bobbed a sort of bow at him.

'We'll step over to the refreshment-room, if you please,' he said. 'We can find a quiet corner there, an' we'll be out o' the way o' the detective fraternity should any of 'em happen ter be about.'

'Aye,' said the Manchester Man.

Without another word exchanged, they made their way through the to-and-fro hurrying crowds to the refreshment room, Val trailing behind. Seated at a little round marble-topped table, the putter-up nervously requested what the Manchester Man would take.

'Pint of Entire.'

Noll Sproggs ordered the same for all three of them without consulting Val. They sat in silence until the waiter had brought the three foam-crowned mugs of beer. Then Noll Sproggs offered a toast.

'Your very good 'ealth.'

The Manchester Man simply took a long silent pull at his tankard. The putter-up passed his tongue across his lips.

'This 'ere young feller's Val,' he said. 'Him as I mentioned in me letter.'

'Oh, aye.'

Val felt sweat spring up on his face.

'Pleased ter meet yer,' he said. Then, feeling this was not adequate, he added : 'Most honoured.'

'I dare say,' the Manchester Man replied, with a look of dry humourless humour.

'Well now,' Noll Sproggs said, after there had been another too long pause. 'Well, first off, is there anything more as you wants ter know? Er – over an' above what I said in the letter?'

'There is.'

'Then ask away, Mr Outhwaite. Ask away.'

'You said nowt about plate-room.'

Val felt a sudden inward sinking at the directness with which the Manchester Man had gone to the one great weakness in all that he had arranged and fought for.

Noll Sproggs shifted in his chair like a boy caught out in a lie.

'No,' he said. 'No, I didn't happen to mention that.'

He at last brought his white face up to look directly at the black-moustached figure opposite him.

'Well, the truth on it is,' he said, 'we come into a bit o' difficulty there. Young Val's the one what runs the maid servant at the 'ouse, an' he's had what you might call a stroke o' bad luck.'

'What stroke?'

Noll Sproggs picked up his beer mug as if he was going to take a long pull, but set it down untasted.

'It's been more'n one thing really,' he said. 'But we got ideas about what – '

'Let him say it.'

Val saw the black-moustached face turn sharply towards him and a pair of cold grey eyes looked at him hard as the barrels of a pair of steadily-held pistols.

He found he was clutching the cool metal of his tankard as if it was a post he needed to cling on to in a gale.

'It – It was goin' a treat ter start with,' he said. 'Goin' a treat. Truly. She was a-singing like a finch in a cage. Only she never 'ad no opportunity ter go into the breakfast-room there. That's where the plate-closet is. Breakfast-room.'

'Get 'er in there.'

'I tried. I tried, honest. But then the butler – Well, all on a sudden 'e took 'er part in a quarrel with the cook. An' – An' then like she wouldn't betray 'im. The butler. Mr Burch.'

'Put 'er on 'er back.'

Val sat blinking. He knew well what he had been so curtly told to do. But the suddenness and the careless brutality of the telling hit at him like a blow.

Defensively he stammered an unnecessary question.

'What — What did you say? Er — sir?'

'Get astride her.'

Now in a rush he sought to justify himself.

'I have. I have. I've done that.'

He thought, for a few withdrawn instants, of that short fumbling instinct-filled spell down that narrow high-walled passageway with Janey, of her fresh willingness, of his own inability to resist what she had insisted on his having.

'You've that much guts then,' the Manchester Man said without any trace of warmth.

'I've guts enough,' Val answered, coming out of his reverie stung to the pitch of overcoming the awe he felt for this toweringly tall, bleakly unmovable man. 'An' I'm ready to —'

'The cook?' the Manchester Man rode like a steam-train over his bluster. 'What's she like?'

'Like?' Val answered, totally checked. 'Well . . . Well, she's the one as made my Janey's life a misery. She's a real —'

'She's not wed?'

Val swallowed.

'Well, they call her Mrs Vickers, but —'

'All cooks is missus. Is there a hubby to be seen?'

'No. No, there ain't so far —'

'Then she'll be a sour bitch. Sour as spoilt milk, take my word. Now, when d'you see this girl o' yourn next?'

'Thursday,' Val jerked out in reply. 'Thursday. Ter-morrer. Or so I hopes.'

'That's summat. Now, you tell her when you see her that if she don't get a good sight o' that plate-closet door, enough to give you all you want to know on it, afore I goes back to wait in Manchester, then you'll make sure as that cook gets to know just what she does in her time-out.'

'But – But –'

But he knew that argument would get him nowhere. He saw even that the brutal treatment which he had been ordered to use – it was a command he had been given, to be obeyed instantly as any order given to a soldier – would in all likelihood swiftly achieve what they had failed to do up till now. Janey, desperate under a threat which would mean desolation in the cold streets for her no less, would blunder somehow into that breakfast-room, risking everything. But even if she were caught and lost her post, her warm if thorny place in the nest, their end would still have been reached. Now that they had hit on the flaw in the character of Policeman Watson they could rely on having time enough to get into No 53 from the front. So all that they still needed in the way of information now was, first and foremost, just how much of an obstacle the plate-closet door was going to be, and, second, the next date on which the Mistress would have her jewels out from the Bank. True, Janey would be their easiest way of getting this last piece of news, but she was not the only way. Noll Sproggs had earlier talked of having used Old Henry on similar affairs, simply to watch the comings and goings at a toffken until he saw a heavy locked box being taken from a cab into the house. So this obstacle could be overcome.

No, once they had found out about the plate-closet door, Janey could be thrown off. And tomorrow she would be waiting for him, surely, at their usual place in Kensington Gardens. And she would wait for two hours and more, he knew, waiting unknowingly for the blow the Manchester Man had so sharply told him to bring down on her.

Val felt himself to be a lone soldier, under orders and beyond any capability of not obeying, whatever he might feel about them.

Janey was at her place under the chestnuts, their spiny leaves now dark and dust-covered, a good quarter of an hour earlier than their usual time. She had had to scamp and scurry through her work to get away and to risk the edge of Mrs Vickers's tongue once again, but she had been determined not to miss a minute of Val if he had got back from Kent as he had said he would.

When she saw him – and only then could she admit to herself that she had known the possibility that she might never see him again – she felt bands break in front of her and she flew across the dark beaten-down grass of summer like a force released.

But he hurried forward and stopped her onrush.

'Janey,' he said, taking her by her out-thrust hands. 'Janey, let's go back there under the trees.'

It was an astonishing thing to say as his first words after four whole long weeks of absence. And she felt astonished to the point of not finding anything to say in reply.

He let fall one of her hands and led her by the other towards the dark shade of the trees.

But then after a few paces she pulled him to a halt.

'No, Val,' she said, not knowing why she felt bound to oppose him but feeling strongly that she did. 'No, let's walk on the path. It's nicer in the sun, an' there's not many about.'

'No,' he answered, with a force that again surprised

and disquieted her. 'No, under the trees.'

She decided to tease him then. It was a weapon she had had in her armoury for only a few weeks, and one she had liked every now and again, when the whim took her, to try out.

'And what would you be wanting with me under the dark o' the trees, I should like to know.'

But Val suddenly thrust his face close to hers. And on it she read, in up-leaping alarm, a black intentness she had by no means expected.

'There was once,' he muttered, his voice thick and urgent, 'when you came with me an' willingly to somewhere dark enough.'

It was as if he had struck her. She drew away with a gasp that had tears in it. He was still holding her by the hand and at her movement his grasp tightened sharply.

'Val, you're hurting.'

'If I let go, will yer come under the trees there and hear what I've to say ter yer?'

'I won't.'

She felt the anger and pride she so often had to suppress in her daily life, the anger and pride that had once not many weeks before felt for a brief minute their hidden strength, break out in her.

But the slaty eyes in Val's face, a face less pale now after the weeks under the Kentish sun, were bitterly intent.

'You won't, won't yer? Then I'll make yer.'

And he began to drag her towards the quiet trees.

'I'll scream. There's a park-keeper over there.'

But she knew that he would well realize the threat was idle.

'You'll come wi' me.'

She allowed herself to be led then. But at every

reluctant pace she asked what it could be that he wanted to say to her. Why was he so intent on getting her to a place far from any onlookers or listeners? What had changed him since she had seen him last?

When, in the leafy light under the tall unswaying chestnuts, he did speak to her, however, his question was so unexpected that she almost laughed aloud in relief.

'Have yer seen the door whilst I was gone?'

For a little she just stood there, fighting the desire to give vent to her feelings in laughter, however near that might be to tears. But then she saw from the unchanged fierce look on his face that this had indeed been what he had dragged her under the trees to ask. And the spirit of protest flamed sharply up.

'What door?' she answered, understanding precisely what he meant but determined to fight him in any way she could.

'You know well what door. The door o' the plate-closet back there. Did yer get ter see it while I was gone?'

'I did not. I said I wanted no more ter do wi' that, an' I don't.'

He looked at her more sharply than ever.

'But you'll go now?' he asked. 'You'll go now an' see it?'

Then his voice took on a crooning note she remembered well, and well remembered how it had always made her weak as melting jelly under him.

'Janey, it's the time now. All that business o' Rosa an' Charlie's forgot now. So you could go an' look at that door easy. And tell me yer will, Janey. Tell me yer will. Janey, it means more nor you could think.'

'I know jus' what it means,' she answered. 'An' I've said already, I ain't a-going ter do it. Mr Burch was kind ter me, kind beyond anything I ever thought 'e could be. An' I won't do that ter 'im. I won't.'

'An' your Mrs Vickers?' he flung out. 'Is she kind now too? An' the Mistress? What about 'er?'

'Well, no, they're same as ever,' she confessed, uneasily feeling herself being forced on to less safe ground. 'But, all the same, Val, I don't – '

'But all the same nothing,' he burst in. 'Janey, you have to be out o' yer bed at five in the mornin' in summer an' yer works till it's time ter go ter bed again. An' what do they do? They get up late an' do nothing but what they like all the day long. You get plain food an' cold often as not. While they have – what did yer tell me? – five separate dishes ter their luncheon an' six ter their dinner. Aye, an' breakfast too an' tea an' supper. Ain't that so, Janey? Ain't it?'

'Yes,' she had to answer. 'It's true enough.'

'Then for God's sake promise me as yer'll go into that breakfast-room tonight.'

But she knew she had a wisdom now that could answer this.

'Val, it's their right ter live like that,' she said, putting all the earnestness she could into it. 'Val, Mr Burch explained it ter me. It's the way it is, Val. They're gentry, Val, an' things is different for gentry.'

She saw the slaty eyes harden.

'Janey, I'm askin' yer ter go into that breakfast-room.'

'No.'

He stood for one instant looking down at her in the greenish light under the fans of leaves above. Then his body tensed like a bent spring.

'Damn yer then, listen ter this. There's plenty o' folk round your way, the servant-maids in the houses near-by, the shopkeepers, plenty who'd like it fine ter be able ter pass on ter Mrs Vickers a cruel word about you.'

She felt understanding pushing its way into her mind.
And fought to stem the seeping tide.

'What cruel word? What about?'

His face looked down on her like an axe-blade.

'About you an' me down that passageway, Janey. Yer
forced me ter say it, an' I've said it. If your Mrs Vickers
knew about that, you'd be out o' No 53 within the
hour. Yer know it. Ain't it so?'

She felt words pass her lips like fragments of broken
glass.

'You. Yer wouldn't. Not you, Val. Oh, Val, yer couldn't
be so 'ard.'

'Janey,' he answered. 'It ain't me. There's someone
– No. No, I must an' I will. Janey, I must an' I do.
I'll tell on yer, Janey, tell on yer so's the word gets back
ter Mrs Vickers quicker nor the wind. Unless yer goes into
that breakfast-room fer me. Unless yer does. So now yer
knows it.'

She saw there was sweat standing on his newly-
browned forehead. But she could not think why. All she
knew was that he had hurt her, hurt her terribly.

There were tears behind her eyes ready to flood out. But
she would not let them. Not in front of him now.

'I don't like yer,' she said, painfully describing with
words she knew to be not the right ones what she was
finding in her heart. 'Val, I don't like yer.'

'Janey,' he answered, begging her. 'Janey, won't yer
do it? Won't yer take a candle tonight an' creep down to
that breakfast-room. Mr Burch'll never hear yer from the
dining-room, not with yer coming down the backstair yer
knows so well. And then, Janey, look at that door.
Note well what it's made on. Is it iron? Or is it wood? If

it's wood, are there panels to it, or not? If it's iron is there a safe-maker's name? Learn that well, Janey. Learn it well an' tell me termorrer, out on the steps. Janey, do it. I'll be waitin' fer yer. At the steps.'

And he swung round and walked fast away, as if he was fighting with himself not to run.

CHAPTER XII

HALF PAST SIX in the morning on Friday the twelfth of July. Northbourne Park Villas almost silent still in the warm morning air. Birds singing. Two streets away the clear slow clopping of a horse and an occasional grating squeal from iron-shod wheels of its cart. Janey out on the steps, as always at this hour, the tools of her trade beside her, broom for sweeping the steps down, rags and jar of polish for the brass of the door, pail of water and hearthstone block for scrubbing the steps at last a milky-white. And she is already kneeling at work on the topmost step, scraping the coarse block back and forth along its water-glistening length, obliterating inch by inch all the footmarks of yesterday. Making ready for the footmarks of today.

And the tears falling, to be lost on the wet stone. Falling unstoppably as she scrubs.

Then, waited-for, expected, but nonetheless cruelly startling, a sound behind her, two words quietly spoken.

'Well, girl?'

Janey swung round on one knee, heart thudding like a clock gone mad, mouth open to gulp in air.

'Oh, Val. You give me such a fright.'

'Yer knew I was goin' ter come,' he answered, leaning well over the gate, speaking very softly, blue-grey eyes darting to and fro. And hard. Hard as stone.

'Yes, yes,' Janey found herself agreeing, whispering as well. 'Yes, I knew. But I didn't dare think what I'd got ter say. I jus kep' me mind on me steps an' the scrubbing.'

She saw his newly-sunburnt face pale with anger.

'So yer didn't go,' he said. 'Yer never went down there an' saw that plate-closet door.'

A fresh spurt of tears welled from her eyes.

'Val,' she pleaded, 'I wanted ter. Or if I didn't, I knew I had ter. An' I was going ter, honest. But I couldn't. I couldn't, Val, there was such ructions in the 'ouse.'

'What ructions?' came the brief brutal question.

'Robert's been dismissed,' she answered. 'The Master found the shutters undone on one o' the library windows. An' he 'ad Robert up in front of 'im, an' created something terrible. An' Robert denied it, an' that made it worse. The Master would've 'ad 'im out o' the 'ouse there an' then, in the middle o' the night, only Mr Burch spoke up fer 'im. But he's going at any minute. Out of it before seven in the morning, Mr Burch promised. An' he's packing 'is things now, an' still swearing 'e didn't never do it an' cussing something terrible, so, Val, I couldn't do nothing about getting into the breakfast-room. They were up till gone one in the morning, an' I'd dropped clean asleep by then. I couldn't 'elp it, Val. I couldn't 'elp meself.'

'Never mind about that. Never mind a penny.'

She sat back on her heels in pure astonishment. What did he mean? Why hadn't he gone for her tooth and nail as she had expected?

And then she saw that the narrow handsome face which she still loved was no longer closed in anger but alight with a quick and blazing joy.

'Val?' she asked.

'Never mind you an' that door,' he answered triumphantly. 'We'll do better nor that by far now. A footman

dismissed from 'is place an' swearing it were unjust, a
servant without a character an' nowhere ter turn. We'll
know every bit about that plate-closet afore the clock's
struck ten. Believe you me.'

The manœuvring forward of many marching columns, the
wheeling of cavalry up to positions of vantage, the slow
dragging into place of the artillery : these are the necessary
preliminaries of battle. They follow a prescribed pattern.
But then, and sometimes swiftly, a gaping weakness in the
defences ahead becomes exposed. It may have sprung from
some gigantic oversight on the part of the General. Or
it may have been due to some culpable omission lower in
the chain of command. Or it may have been no more
than the effect of chance during the heat of the engage-
ment. But, whatever the cause, the question is : will the
advancing force be able to seize the opportunity created?
Or will the sudden chance simply be looked at stupidly,
with a feeling that such things ought not to happen and
therefore have not happened, and thus be left unexploited?
The answer depends often on the qualities and character of
one man at one place.

When Val Leary, furiously listening to Janey's blubber-
ing excuses, had heard that Robert had been dismissed he
could have let the news pass over him as so much
unimportant side-matter. But his honed predatory instinct,
product of years of privation married to an inborn strength
of will, seized at once on the significance of the chance
information.

Robert would be vengeful. Robert would be feeling
acutely his lack of money. Robert would be ripe for
exploitation.

And all that Val had to do, when he had abruptly left Janey, was to station himself in a convenient hiding-place, the nook he had watched from before where a thick-trunked sycamore grew on the pavement close to the wall of a house on the far side from No 53 about half-way along, and there wait. He had not been in place a quarter of an hour when he saw the tall figure of Robert emerge from the area of No 53, a large sagging wicker hamper on his shoulder. He watched just long enough to see which way he went, and then he set off himself in the opposite direction.

Smiling like a fox, he ran at a good steady pace down to the first turning, round it, along to the next street, the one parallel to Northbourne Park Villas, and up this as fast as he could go. Then he cut across, still running but up on silent toes, and he was waiting, sitting cheerfully at ease on the wall round St Stephen's Church, when a chap much his own age came staggering along in the early-morning quiet carrying on his shoulder a large and sagging wicker hamper.

'Give yer a hand wi' that, mate?'

And it was done. Some friendly talk as they walked, each holding the big hamper by a handle. A drink suggested. A tale poured out. Mysterious assistance promised. The hamper taken on to the servants' lurk in Paddington that Robert had told Mr Burch would be his temporary stopping-place. A visit set in hand to a gin-shop in Newel Street, Soho.

A good General when he learns that a dangerous gap has been opened in his defences will spare nothing to take appropriate counter-measures. A bad General will persist in a course because he has ordered it, and be damned to the breach which that course has left open, however wide and evident.

Mortimer Johnson was neither bad nor good. He was a human being, endowed by fate or the chance of progress over the generations of the family he sprang from with considerable responsibilities. These he enjoyed to the full, though he was often conscious that they were responsibilities. Yet, being human, there were occasions when he abused the power that the accident of birth had placed in his hands. He let the ill-temper he had inherited or acquired have vent more often, much more often, than there was any real excuse for. And in the house no one was more calculated to rouse his ill-sleeping ire than Miss Christopher, whose obsessive tentativeness seemed exactly calculated to enrage him.

Miss Christopher, one of the two people whose presence in the household at No 53 Northbourne Park Villas Janey had not ever spoken of to Val, never having dared admit that when they had first spent time together in Kensington Gardens she had been ready to pander to a spoilt child's insistence on having his bedtime hot milk and cinnamon prepared by no other hands than hers.

Miss Christopher, who came very seldom into contact with Robert, the footman, hardly other in fact than on those rare occasions when Robert, by chance a little early laying the breakfast-table, found her in the room and sometimes noticed that one of the sugar-bowls contained fewer lumps than he had put into it not long before.

Miss Christopher, whom Robert when he thought of her at all thought of simply as a creature to despise, and whom therefore he was quite unlikely to mention at the gin-shop in Newel Street venting his spleen there against the gentry of No 53 Northbourne Park Villas.

K

Miss Christopher and her charge, Frederick.

Miss Christopher, standing now straight-backed, stiff and rustling in her black, with her features held and held in a mask of severity, outside the tall mahogany door of the library, to which between nine and half past every morning Mr Mortimer Johnson was wont to retire with the *Morning Post*. Miss Christopher, her veined and skinny hand firmly clasping little Frederick's child-soft wrist. And Frederick fearfully, appallingly red in the face.

'No, Frederick, you must come with me this moment and tell your father.'

'I don't want to.'

A declaration, all will, all opposition, all belief that fury in the end always got you out of any sort of unpleasantness. But now fury has more to overcome than it has ever had yet in eight years of trial.

'Frederick, you must come,' Miss Christopher replied, forcing her voice like her features into an alien implacability. 'That thoughtless act of yours in opening those shutters got Robert into very serious trouble.'

'Wasn't thoughtless.'

Miss Christopher looked down at the set sulky mutinous face and sighed.

'Yes, Frederick, it was thoughtless.'

'It wasn't. It wasn't. I thought about it, didn't I? I thought I heard a fire-engine going along the street, and I thought I would go into the library to look at it because I knew Papa was having his dinner.'

'Yes, and you should not have done so, Frederick. You had been put to bed, and it was your duty to stay there. You know that. Well, you did wrong, and now you must tell your father.'

The small face plainly replaced fury with cunning.

'But, Miss Christopher, I told you that I did it.'

She did not loosen her grasp on that soft wrist despite the slackening of the tantrum pull which had filled her with a dreadful fear of being toppled off her feet. This time she would impose her will. This time there was injustice to another, to someone other than herself, to be taken into account.

'Yes, Frederick, you did tell me, and I am glad, truly glad, that you owned up to your wrongdoing. But now you must be yet more of a little man and admit to your father what you have done.'

'But – But he'll beat me, Miss Christopher.'

From underneath the fury-filled creature, and from underneath the cunning one, there peeped the terror-stricken. She felt pity tug at her as hard as until a moment before she had been tugged at physically. But she forced her mind back to remembering what her duty was.

'No. Your father must be told.'

Then in an instant Frederick was back to heaving and writhing for escape. But she was determined to stand her ground and she dug her heels into the thick pile of the rug under them and leant backwards and held him. She held him long enough to feel the tugging slacken, to be able to reach across to the forbidding polished mahogany door and to knock on it. To knock more loudly and more abruptly than she would have wished to.

'What – What – Who's there?'

The voice inside sounded startled and at once filled with irritation. Mr Johnson, it was well known in the house, did not like to be disturbed during this quiet half-hour. But her knuckles had rapped against the hard wood – and been hurt in doing so – and the voice had answered.

And there was no going back now. She turned the chased brass knob and pushed the door open, dragging behind her a scuffling Frederick, suddenly and heart-rendingly white-faced.

'Good – Good morning, Mr Johnson,' she said, at once regretting her stupidity when she had already wished him good morning not an hour earlier at Prayers, as she always did and seldom gained acknowledgement for.

'What is it, ma'am?'

Mr Johnson looked up at her from his paper, bringing his eyebrows furiously together. Nothing which she had entered the room to tell him, that bar of interlocked prickly hair seemed to say, could possibly justify such an intrusion.

She braced herself again.

'Sir, it is Frederick. I have brought him to you. There is something he wishes to tell you.'

'Hmph. I doubt, ma'am, whether this can conceivably be the time for childish affairs. I should already have left for the City, and I would have been gone had it not been for that disgraceful business last night.'

Miss Christopher felt flooded with a sense of her own ill-advised behaviour. She did not dare to look at the clock on the mantel, though she could have been certain that the time was not much after a quarter-past nine, well before Mr Johnson's habitual hour of departure. But in the wrong or in the right, what she had to force Frederick to say had to be embarked upon.

'Yes. Yes, sir,' she heard herself gabble. 'But it was – It is indeed concerning the – the business last night that Frederick wishes to speak to you.'

'What? What is all this?'

Until now the *Morning Post* had remained most of the

time up in front of Mr Johnson's face. But now he lowered it to his knees.

'I trust,' he said, 'that Frederick has not come to plead for that man Robert. The fellow had not been allowed to spoil the boy, had he?'

Miss Christopher met the accusing glare full on.

'I – I hope I would never permit a servant to do that,' she managed to say.

'No?'

Mr Johnson had seemed momentarily disconcerted. But he took an angry survey of his small son.

'Well, let the boy speak for himself.'

And Frederick became unable to speak. Miss Christopher felt she could see the words he ought to be saying sticking in his throat like the pieces of gristly meat that so often fell to her portion at the luncheon-table and which she found so hard to swallow and yet did not like to leave untouched on her plate.

'Well, boy, have you lost your tongue?'

The words were hardly calculated to be reassuring.

'No.' A long-stretching pause. 'No, Papa, I –'

Breakdown.

'Come, what nonsense is this?'

'Papa, it was me. I did it.'

Miss Christopher felt a washing spread of relief. She had taken a firm line, knowing for once that it was right. And firmness had at last brought the desired end.

But she had reckoned without Frederick's father.

'Did it? Did it? Did what?'

He wheeled to her.

'For heaven's sake, ma'am, have you not taught the boy how to speak?'

For a moment she felt battered into incapability of

speech herself. Then she brought out the necessary words.

'Frederick, tell your father just what it was that you did.'

And at last Frederick pushed himself over the obstacle, and the words came pouring out.

'The shutters. It was me. I left them open when I'd gone to watch a fire-engine go by. Papa, it wasn't Robert.'

Miss Christopher, lifted from depths to heights once more, drew herself up with a shiver of pride.

'As soon as little Frederick confessed to me, sir,' she said, 'I brought him to you. I realized you would want to send out for Robert as soon as possible.'

And she was rewarded with a glare of purpling rage.

'I knew it, ma'am. You did bring the boy here to plead with me. I cannot conceive what malign spirit has entered into members of this household. First it is Burch presuming to tell me that it is my duty to keep an acknowledged thief under my roof. And now it is you, coming to me with this canting, mollycoddling, lily-livered claptrap.'

Miss Christopher dimly saw then that you do not disturb the order of the universe without provoking rage in the heavens.

'Mr Johnson,' she said, endeavouring to hold up to this storm a tattered frail-spoked umbrella. 'Sir, what Frederick told you is – It is no more than the simple truth.'

'Nonsense, woman,' came the answer in thunder. 'It was Robert's duty to close those shutters. I myself came in and found them open behind the curtains. You will please not question decisions which I have taken.'

'But – But, Mr Johnson,' she persisted, a heedless lemming running to destruction. 'Frederick has told you that it was he who opened the shutters after Robert closed them. It was a thoughtless act, but – '

Mr Johnson leapt up from his chair.

'I will not have this,' he blared. 'I have dismissed that man. And you – I suppose that you are now asking me to go down on my bended knee to the fellow and beg him to come back.'

'But, sir, if he was dismissed because of something which was no fault of his, then – '

'No fault of his? Are you telling me that I was wrong to dismiss one of my own servants?'

Miss Christopher felt herself falter. The lemming lifted for an instant its head and saw the watery deep ahead.

'I – I am not saying that you were wrong, of course, Mr Johnson. It is – It is just that I . . .'

But she could say no more.

In her employer's eye she saw a gleam of new ferocity appear.

'It is just, ma'am, that you are prey to a flood of soft-hearted poppycock. And now, if you please, I am long overdue leaving for the City. So good day to you, ma'am. Good day. And let us hear no more of this matter. Now, or at any other time. Good day.'

'Good day, sir,' said Miss Christopher.

She turned and walked across to the tall mahogany door, opened it, ushered Frederick through in front of her and went out.

But beyond the door Frederick, who amid the thunder and the lightning had kept quiet as a rain-soaked mouse, filled out in an instant to his old indulged tyrannical self. Miss Christopher saw in his eyes the pure unalloyed scorn of childhood.

'Well,' he said, in clearly ringing tones, 'you didn't make Papa take Robert back, did you?'

CHAPTER XIII

THE FINAL ASSAULT on the house at No 53 Northbourne Park Villas, London West, took place in the early hours of July the twenty-third, Tuesday, ten days after the dismissal of Robert, the footman.

Robert had sung to Noll Sproggs at Newel Street. How he had sung. He had confirmed everything Janey had ever told Val about the household. And, without any difficulty at all, he had been able to give the putter-up a full and complete description of the door to the plate-closet. What he had not happened to refer to, since the subject had not chanced to arise in all the talk, was that the fourth of Mr Mortimer Johnson's sons, little Frederick, was not away at school like his brothers but was in the house together with his nervous, sugar-stealing, Charlotte Yonge-reading governess, Miss Christopher.

Robert had been able to provide, too, one additional piece of information which Val had not acquired from Janey: the fact that on the coming Monday week Mr and Mrs Johnson were to attend the opera and that for the occasion Mrs Johnson would naturally have her full complement of jewellery sent round from the bank. It was this piece of knowledge that had set the date for Noll Sproggs and caused him at once to telegraph to a certain address in Manchester saying 'Infant expected July twenty-second. All well.'

So Val had had two Thursdays on which to persuade Janey to come round again to his way of thinking. And it was important to secure her consent once more because,

whether Val wished it or not, she had been allocated
a part in the affair.

It was going to be her task to counter what had come to
be the greatest obstacle remaining : the sleeping presence in
the dining-room, just across from the breakfast-room with
its plate-closet, of Mr Burch on his camp-bed, gooseshot-
loaded gun beside him.

Val had anxiously posed the problem to Noll Sproggs
long before, when he had first learnt from Janey about this
newest precaution the Master had put in train at No 53.

'Mr Sproggs, what we going ter do about it? That
old Mr Burch'll wake, Mr Sproggs, come on us unawares
with that shotgun . . .'

'There's ways, lad.'

'But what, Mr Sproggs?'

'Why, a bit o' rope. That's the most as you'll need. A bit
o' rope, lad, strung from the 'andle o' that dining-room
door across to the doorknob opposite, or to yer newel-post
on the stair if so be that comes handier. Then if 'e do
wake, 'e finds 'e can't pull the door open, 'e kicks up a
row an' the pair on yer 'as plenty o' time ter mizzle. Or
there's the wedges.'

'The wedges?'

'Yer puts a leather wedge hard up against the door
o' each room as yer workin' in, lad. Never forget 'em.
Give yer a good two minute if yer palled, they do.'

'Yes, Mr Sproggs.'

But it had been the Manchester Man, when they were
seeing him off on his way home again after his whirlwind
visit, who had curtly said what was actually to be done
when the bust took place.

'What you doing about the butler in that dining-
room?' he had asked the putter-up.

'Rope across the door.'

'No.'

'There's the wedges. They're good the – '

'I want him out o' the road, not wakin' and hollerin'.'

'Ah, yes. That'd be the best. That'd be the best, certainly. Only how's it – '

'Summat in his cocoa. Most o' his sort take a cup o' cocoa last thing. Get that girl to put summat in. Armstrong's Black Drops'd do, if yer don't stint.'

So Armstrong's Black Drops, that strong stand-by patent medicine, had been agreed on. And now had come the time to persuade Janey to use it.

Val left it on the first Thursday almost till the very end. For all the afternoon and the evening, when they had gone to a penny gaff and there had been no chance amid the singing of the songs and the shouts and cheers for the dumbshow-play to talk, he had steered clear of anything which might at all remind Janey of the bust. But at last, strolling towards Northbourne Park Villas through the soft darkness, he knew the time had come.

'We 'eard from Robert that they're a-going ter the opery Monday week,' he said, breaking into the warm silence that there had been between them.

Janey came to a halt.

'I knew yer was thinking on it.'

It was an accusation. He put all he knew into creating a defence.

'Janey,' he said, lapping his voice round her. 'Janey, it's my chance. My chance as I've waited fer all me life, as I've worked nigh on four months fer. The only chance as I'll 'ave in this world ter better meself.'

'But, Val – '

'No. Janey, it's not ter better meself only. It's ter better the both on us. Janey, what chance 'ave you got, any more than me? What are yer there, at No 53? Kitchen-maid. An' what else will yer be?'

'Well, I could get ter be 'ousemaid, if may be Maggie leaves or something.'

'An' is she so much better off nor you?'

'Well, no, she ain't. But there's girls as 'as started off as kitchen-maid and rose up ter be professed cook. I knows there is. Mrs Vickers is always telling me.'

'An' are you going ter do that?'

'I might.'

'Yer won't. Yer knows yer won't. What've you learnt so far in all the time you been in the 'ouse? You was telling me once: that Mrs Vickers, when she's making one o' her special sauces that they likes up there, won't so much as let yer near the stove.'

'Well, she says they're 'er secret, what she depends on.'

'Aye, depends on ter keep you down.'

He saw that the thrust had gone home. And he followed it up hard.

'Janey, listen ter me. If you shares in the night's work what's coming, then you'll share in what's got out of it. Janey, if I'm a-doing this ter better meself, I'm a-doing it ter better you too.'

'But I don't know as – '

'Listen, girl. You'll 'ave ter wait a bit, o' course. 'Twouldn't never do fer a servant girl in a 'ouse ter want ter leave just a week arter a bust. Detective-officers'd be round 'er ears in a twinkling. But, you wait yer bit, my Janey, an' then you'll see.'

'Would I, Val?'

And he knew then that she yearned to hear what he could place in front of her. He filled his mind with that picture of what might be, of what she would most like to be.

'Janey, I'll tell yer. Give in yer notice, maybe arter a couple o' month, maybe arter a week or two more ter be on the safe side. An' by then I'll 'ave 'ad me share. Oh, it won't be a quarter nor yet a fifth o' the pickings we'll get. Those as 'as been in the business longer gets the big slices. An' we won't get from the fencers 'alf, no, nor a quarter, o' the value o' the plate an' the jewels. But, never you mind, there'll be enough left at the end on it. Enough fer me an' you, Janey. In some little business, with a place of our own above. Eh, Janey? Sitting together by a snug little fire in winter, maybe out in a bower of scarlet beans in summer. What yer think? D'yer like it? D'yer like the thought o' that?'

There was scarcely any need for him to hear her answer. It showed clearly in her eyes, shining up at him wide and open, in the faint gleam of the lamplight.

'Oh, Val, will it be so?'

'It will be, Janey mine. So an' always so.'

'Then I'm with yer, Val. I'm with yer, whether I wants ter be or no.'

Half past eight in the evening of July the twenty-second. No lamp lit in Noll Sproggs's back parlour, though dusk was deepening with every minute in the cloudless sky outside. The sole low window let in enough light but, fast closed as always, there came through it no breeze to cool the baking heat left by the long summer's day now drawing to its close.

In the little airless room there was the putter-up himself, sitting in his customary wooden-armed chair drawn up to the table, there was Val, on a hard wooden-backed chair turned reverse way round with his arms folded across the top and his chin on them, there was Old Henry, close by the putter-up, looking pointedly every now and again towards the black gin-bottle on the table, and there was Eileen.

Eileen had been a full party to the affair for only three days. It had happened simply enough. The girl Noll Sproggs employed regularly as a canary, to carry innocently to the scene of a bust the give-away tools of the cracksman's trade, had come down with a fever. Val had chanced to be at the gin-shop when the girl's mother had told Noll Sproggs and he had promptly offered Eileen in her place. He had regretted the impulse immediately afterwards, when he realized that it might mean bringing Eileen and Janey together. But by then the putter-up had seized on the offer – 'She's gone on yer, she won't prove no blabber' – and it was too late. He felt sharply uneasy that the two girls would no longer be kept as far as possible apart, both in his mind, as he preferred it, and in actual fact, when any meeting between them would be almost certainly disastrous. But there was nothing to be done about it, and, as the appointed Monday night drew nearer and nearer the excitement he felt, and the edge of fear, blotted out every other thought.

'Well,' said Old Henry, quite suddenly in the little close airless room, breaking a long nerve-stretching silence, 'time fer me ter be off.'

He pushed his chair back with a dull scrape on the floor and eyed the gin-bottle one last time, unsuccessfully.

He turned to Val.

'An' don't yer ferget me calls,' he said. 'The terrier a

yap-yap-yapping fer a light going on unexpected inside, the whine of a bitch on heat fer danger outside, an' the three long cat-yowls fer yer all-clear.'

'You've told me often enough,' Val answered.

'Aye, but you'll ferget. Mark my words.'

'If 'e do,' Noll Sproggs put in, 'there's one o' the party as'll not.'

But the oblique mention of the Manchester Man, waiting at this moment in a cheap hotel close by the station at Euston for Val in due course to come and collect him, did not seem to cheer the putter-up as much as it might have done.

'An' the cabbie,' Old Henry said, at the door, settling his rusty black stovepipe even lower on to his head. 'He'll not ferget 'is false plates?'

' 'Ave yer ever known 'im fail?' Noll Sproggs answered, with a touch of irritability at doubt cast on a system he had told Val he always used, as a four-wheeler drew less attention at night by far than a coster-cart with its load mysteriously covered or two men carrying bulging sacks.

'I s'pose not.'

And with that concession to the optimistic, Old Henry set out. Till dawn he would watch over the house at No 53, flitting from one dark nook to another, each carefully selected weeks before. He would wait and watch, ready to note the least alteration in the regular routine, the least sign that all was not as counted on.

When at last the little door into the bar had been slowly closed behind the crow's rusty-black stooped figure no one said anything in the parlour. But a thought filled Val's mind like a dark boulder in a bowl of water – and he knew that the others must be thinking the same thing

— 'Now it's begun.'

Mr Burch customarily took his cocoa at a quarter to ten each night, in time to have it in comfort before setting off at ten to make sure that all the outer doors of the house were bolted as well as locked and that all the windows were properly shuttered. It was Janey's duty to prepare the drink for him.

A quarter of an hour later she prepared more for Mrs Vickers, who liked to take her cocoa in the twenty minutes or so before she made her way up to her room. As soon as Janey had brought her the steaming cup she herself was expected to go off to bed as quickly as might be.

Just before half past nine on the night of Monday, July the twenty-second, she was to be found standing in the scullery, alone in the semi-darkness. Only a beam of light from the kitchen, coming in through the just-open door, gave any illumination. But Janey did not need light. Not for thinking.

Armstrong's Black Drops. Armstrong's Black Drops. The words ran and ran in her head.

The little bottle Val had given her, of thick glass about three inches tall and less than an inch across, was in her pocket. As she stood there, hands spread out at her waist, she could feel its hard shape. There had been no label on it, though there were signs that one had been torn off. She could guess why. If she was caught with it, or if it was found when she had thrown it away afterwards as Val had told her to do, no one would know what it was. She would say it was something she had got for her stomach. In summer you often needed something.

But I won't ever need to tell them, her thoughts crystallized abruptly. In five minutes, less, I'm going to put it all in his cocoa.

Armstrong's Black Drops. What if they should turn out to be too strong? Was Val telling the tale about them? He could have given me something as'd do harm. He might. He was hard sometimes. Hard. The way he talked about the toffs in the Gardens of a Thursday. What if he has given me something as'll really hurt Mr Burch? Mr Burch was so good to me that time. And other times too.

She scrabbled into her pocket and for a moment in the darkness took out the little bottle.

Pour it all down the sink. Tell Val I did give them to Mr Burch, and not do it. Val'll never know the difference. Or will he? What if Mr Burch wakes up when they come? Hears them? Comes out with that gun? Perhaps then there won't be any Val to see next Thursday.

She pushed the bottle deep as it would go back into her pocket.

But do I want Val to come, him and the others? Wouldn't it be better far if he got scared off before he'd hardly begun? I don't want the place burgled. It's my place, too. I'm in this house. That's what Mr Burch says. We're all together. And it's true.

But Mrs Vickers. That cow. She in with me? She ain't, you know. She blinking well ain't. Making me scrub the floor in the kitchen twice this morning. Just because she took it into her head that she could see a streak of dirt right under the table. 'Scrub that floor, my girl. Scrub it every inch, and this time scrub it right.' Cow. Cow. Cow. I hope Val does come and prig every blessed thing in the house. I hope he does. I hope he does. I hope he does.

Hand in her pocket firmly clutching the little bottle of dark liquid, Janey marched out of the scullery into the well-lit kitchen and the stove awaiting her. With her back to the room, as she stood to watch the milk boil in the pan, she told herself, no one could ever see her slip the drops in. No one would.

'Chisel,' called Noll Sproggs, seated at the table in his snug parlour, the shutters on its window now securely locked.

Val, standing over a miscellaneous heap of objects piled on the threadbare carpet, picked out a chisel and handed it up to Eileen.

'Chisel,' he said.

Eileen took the tool, its edge gleaming from recent careful sharpening on the oilstone, and wrapped it in the corner of a sack taken from a pile on a chair beside her.

'Saw,' Noll Sproggs called.

'Saw.'

Val took up a sturdy-bladed saw and handed it in its turn to be wrapped in the sack.

'Hammer. Got the muffle on firm, 'as it?'

Val pulled at the double-layered leather muffle tied with fine cord round the hammer-head.

'Firm as can be.'

Eileen added the tool to the others in the sack, bundled all three carefully together and placed them in a large carpet-bag that stood in the exact centre of the putter-up's round table.

'Cutter,' called Noll Sproggs.

Selecting the implement from the pile, Val thought of the time it had taken him to master it. All afternoon a week ago he had tried pushing its central spike into an old piece of flat wood and then working its turning-bar round and round so that the thinner cutting spike moved in

L

a circle over the wood, gradually splintering its way
deeper in until at last it had cut a complete hole. It had
been hard work. And there had been a knack to master
too, contriving to hold the whole tool steady so that the
cutting spike was kept hard in its groove. And it had
been noisy work. The thought of making that splintery
tearing sound in the dead of night was enough to bring
the sweat up. But it would have to be done. And not so
long from now either.

'Cutter.'

He handed the awkward thing to Eileen for wrapping in
its own particular sack.

'Silent lights.'

'Silent lights.'

Up to Eileen went the stout matches that were so much
more expensive than ordinary lucifers, and so much less
noisy to strike.

'Tapers.'

He selected the coil of white tapers, noting how Noll
Sproggs had bought the very best.

'Tapers.'

'Dark-lantern.'

'Dark-lantern.'

He handed up the little blackish lantern with the
shutter that had one tiny hole in it to let out a ray of light
no bigger than a penny.

'Mind 'ow yer stows that, girl,' the putter-up said in his
hoarse voice. 'There's oil in it. An' you, lad, mind 'ow yer
'olds it when you're in there. It gets 'ot as 'ell pretty
quick, an' we don't want yer a-dropping of it.'

'I'll remember.'

'Wedges, one dozen.'

'Wedges,' Val said, picking out the bundle of leather

door-wedges tied together on a loop, and wondering, not for the first time, whether Janey had given that butler the Black Drops. It was past his cocoa time now. Had she managed it? Or had she suddenly decided against the whole thing? It was so chancy. So damned chancy. But no other way for it.

'Pair o' masks. An' see yer keeps yours on, young 'un. If yer gets your features seen, yer could be traced back to 'ere.'

Val selected the two coarse black cotton masks with their crudely-cut eyeholes. They would be devilish hot to wear on a night like this.

'Pair o' masks,' he said.

'Two dozen assorted betties.'

He handed the big bunch of picklocks to Eileen for swaddling.

'Two dozen betties.'

'An' you give those ter 'im,' Noll Sproggs said, as if he preferred to avoid mentioning the Manchester Man by name. 'He'll know ter take care on 'em. I 'ad a set left in a 'ouse once, an' they cost me near on a quarter of all we got out of 'er. Not that these ain't worth it, whatever they cost. 'Cos if one o' them don't open up the lockfast in the bedroom sweet as oil, then I'm a Dutchman.'

He watched while Eileen wrapped the precious set in a piece of rag and deposited the bundle safely in one corner of the carpet-bag.

'Pair o' curling-tongs same as used by me own dear wife, if I 'ad one.'

'Pair o' tongs.'

These too Val had practised with, shut by Noll Sproggs into a room at the top of the gin-shop and made to twist and wriggle the tongs' long shafts till they turned the butt-end of the key left in the lock and let him out.

'American auger.'

'Auger, an' two, three, four, five, six bits.'

He handed up the clumsily-shaped brace with its bits tied to it with a strip of cloth.

'Peter-cutter.'

'Peter-cutter.'

'An' there's another as yer wants ter keep a good watch on. Best Birmingham manufacture. Can go through yer iron safe-door like a di'mond cuts glass, that can. An' cost accordin'.'

'I'll look arter it.'

'Two balls o' twine.'

There was nothing else left on the floor. Val picked up the balls of twine and handed them to Eileen to wedge as they were into the carpet-bag.

'That's the lot then,' Noll Sproggs said. ' 'Cepting these.'

From the pockets of his coat he pulled two long sausage-shaped objects made of sailcloth and evidently, from their floppiness, remarkably heavy.

'What's them, Mr Sproggs?' Eileen asked.

'Eel-skins, me dear,' said the putter-up, the smallest bit more easygoing than usual now that things were at last moving. 'That's what we calls 'em. Eel-skins.'

'But what they for?'

The gooseberry-green eyes looked across at her.

'Ter keep folk quiet, that's what.'

Eileen drew back.

'I – I don't much care for the like o' that,' she said.

'Sometimes known as the life-preserver, me dear,' the putter-up answered equably. 'Ter preserve the life o' your fancy-boy on this occasion. If so be as they're found necessary.'

He dropped the two sandbags in with the rest of the gear and picked up from the pile of sacks an old red cotton gown which he then carefully folded and placed in the top of the bag so that it hid the rest of the contents from any chance inspection. At last he shut the clasp with a loud click.

'So that's that,' he said.

CHAPTER XIV

THE MILK in the pan on the kitchen stove began to rise.

'Janey.'

Janey jumped like a hare at the sudden sound behind her. Waiting for some moment to pick itself as the right one in which to slip into the pan the contents of the heavy little bottle in her pocket, she had been so intent on the wrinkling creamy-white surface of the milk that she had forgotten the existence of the world at her back.

She darted a scared glance behind her.

It was Mr Burch. Mr Burch standing, not close by, thank goodness, but on the far side of the big kitchen table.

'Yes, Mr Burch?' she stammered out.

'Keep an eye on that pan, don't let it boil over.'

'No, sir. No.'

She turned back and took the pan off the heat.

'I just stepped in to say that since it is so extremely close tonight I think I shall forgo my cocoa this once.'

'Yes, Oh, yes, Mr Burch.'

Janey felt as if, stepping on to what she had believed to be a solid flagstone, it had slowly floated away beneath her. She did not know whether to be delighted that she could no longer give Mr Burch the Black Drops or whether to feel furious that the scheme she had promised to play her part in had been ruined at a casual stroke.

'Set the pan aside, girl. You can use the milk for Mrs Vickers's cocoa later on.'

'Yes, sir. Yes, Mr Burch.'

Noll Sproggs broke the silence that had settled once more

on the stuffy little room with its darkly-shining cupboarded walls.

'We'll give yer a drop o' brandy, boy,' he said. 'Nothing like yer French brandy ter set up the spirits for a night's work ter come.'

'Thank yer, Mr Sproggs,' Val answered, abruptly feeling a sinking that perhaps French brandy would counter.

'Yerss.'

Slowly the putter-up pushed himself out of his chair, went across to one of the cupboards, unlocked it with a key from the bunch he pulled from his waistcoat pocket, took out a bottle three-parts filled with fine light brown liquid and two small glinting and gleaming glasses. He poured a small measure of the liquid into each glass, handed one to Val and lifted his own in a toast.

'To the night ahead.'

Val gulped.

'The night ahead,' he responded.

Eileen, sitting in a corner, the heavy carpet-bag at her feet, joined wordlessly in the toast in the glass of rum and milk she had been nursing for the past three-quarters of an hour.

Silence descended again on the little airless room.

Janey had begun to make cocoa for Mrs Vickers at precisely her usual time, using the milk she had set aside when Mr Burch had so unexpectedly decided not to have his customary hot drink.

The milk was already rimmed with little solid bubbles.

Should she tip the Black Drops in? She put her hand on the small round bottle in her pocket. But the milk came up in the pan with a swoosh at that moment and she had to snatch it off the heat to stop it boiling over.

She allowed that to decide her. She would put the drops down the WC on her way to bed. Mrs Vickers could go free. And Mr Burch had already escaped. But what if he did wake when they came . . .

Yet could this really be the night, she asked herself. It did not somehow seem possible that the calm and regular ways of the house were about to be brutally torn apart. And if Mr Burch woke, wouldn't that be the best thing in the end? If he scared them away with that gun and no more was heard of it?

'Janey.'

It was Mr Burch again. But this time, with the decision about the Black Drops safely past, the voice coming from behind did not scare her. She turned, took the milk pan over to the table and poured its contents with a steady hand into Mrs Vickers's cup.

'Yes, Mr Burch?'

She gave him a smile, as she often did now that she understood him more.

'Didn't Mrs Vickers make some lemonade this afternoon?'

'Yes, Mr Burch. She said as 'ow seeing it was so 'ot she thought they might like it.'

'And did they? I never took any up.'

'No, Mr Burch. Rosa mentioned it to the Mistress, but she said she hadn't asked for any to be made and wouldn't 'ave it.'

'I see. Well, I think in that case I'll take some myself. I'll have to wait up till they come back from the opera, and it will pass the time. Bring me a small jug to the servants' hall. I hope it's good and strong.'

'Yes. Yes, it is, Mr Burch. The way Mrs Vickers always

makes it, so's you can really taste the lemons.'

Eileen set out for Northbourne Park Villas at eleven o'clock exactly, lugging the weighty carpet-bag. She walked at a good pace, despite the heavy-lying heat. Towards the end of Oxford Street, within a hundred yards of the Marble Arch, she encountered a pair of patrolling policemen. The sight of them sent a new flush of sweat running down all her body. But she kept steadily on. And when she reached them they gave her scarcely a glance, plainly seeing no more than a young woman making her way home from a visit.

At just before midnight Mr and Mrs Johnson reached No 53 in the carriage. John, the coachman, waited till he had seen Burch open the door before taking the carriage round to the mews. Burch offered his Master and Mistress a cold collation, which he said he had set out in the dining-room. But they told him that it was much too hot to eat anything and that they would go straight to bed.

Old Henry, stuffed like a bundle of black cloth into the narrow gap between the wall of the house midway along Northbourne Park Villas and the thick old sycamore just outside it, from where he could see clearly if at an oblique angle the whole of the front of No 53, noted the succession of lights in the windows coming on and being extinguished. One by one he drew the correct conclusions as to what was taking place inside.

'Sweet dreams an' many,' he murmured when at length the crack of light showing through the curtains of Mr and Mrs Johnson's second-floor bedroom disappeared.

'Sweet dreams an' many.'

At one o'clock exactly Val met Eileen at the place chosen for them by Old Henry. It was the narrow high-walled passageway some five or ten minutes' walk from Northbourne Park Villas where Janey had on the last night in May given Val a gift he had not at all expected.

Val had left the Manchester Man in the Bayswater Road where the two of them had got down from the cab that had brought them from the hotel at Euston, Val's first taste of such a luxury. The Manchester Man was to walk to the far end of Northbourne Park Villas from No 53, there to meet Old Henry and hear if all was well. Val, in the meanwhile, had walked on his own to this spot.

He had not much liked the thought of his destination.

He would have wished to be meeting Eileen in any place but that. Yet he had known he could not say to Noll Sproggs, when the passageway had first been selected, that he did not want to go there because it was where he and Janey had made love. Nevertheless the place seemed to bring together the two parts of his life like two laden craft propelled by opposing currents and heading for inevitable shipwreck.

His steps had gradually grown slower as he had approached, but at last they brought him to the entrance to the passage, its two high walls running into almost impenetrable darkness.

'Eileen,' he called cautiously.

A paler shape moved out of the blackness of the passage towards him.

'Sssh. Yes, it's me.'

'All's well?'

She was beside him now, his Eileen, his own Eileen.

'Sure,' she said. 'An' why wouldn't all be well? Who's to take notice o' a poor working-girl an' her ol' carpet-bag? An' you? Is all well with you?'

'Yes, yes. Right as rain.'

He wondered whether he did sound confident. But she seemed satisfied. Thank goodness she had come up to the entrance of the passageway and not expected him to go down it. To have stood there and talked with her where . . .

But they must not linger. Should some passer-by chance to see a girl handing a heavy carpet-bag to a fellow they might ask themselves what it was all about.

'Give it ter me then,' he said.

She swung the bag towards him and he took it.

'Good luck so,' she whispered.

He thought then for the first time of what task she still had to do for them.

'An' the best o' luck to you too,' he said. 'To you an' your Policeman No 126, if yer finds 'im.'

She laughed then. A low throaty sound in the heat-laden darkness.

'Sure, an' I'll find him,' she said. 'An' I'll keep him too, just as long as you want safe there in front o' No 53.'

'Do it,' Val said, suddenly doubting if it was as easy as they had counted on. 'Do it, for we'll not get in there without one gap in the feller's round.'

'You'll get in.'

Abruptly her confidence sent a gust of irritation through him. With her standing almost, as it seemed, in Janey's very shoes, he was ready to fire up at anything.

'Aye,' he said bitterly. 'You'll find 'im an' you'll keep 'im, but what'll yer have ter do ter make sure o' that?'

'I'll do what's needed,' she answered calmly. 'That an' no more.'

'An' you'll like the doing of it too,' he flung at her.

'Whist now,' she said. 'Yer knows well I'll not do that. Yer knows well there's only one chap in the whole wide world fer me, an' that's the chap as I met in the Whiffler one day long ago in the spring.'

There could be no doubting she meant the words. He let a silence pass. Then he sighed. If only there had been no Janey. And there was a lass who was going to be bitter-hearted enough when this night's work was finished with.

'Good luck at last,' he said, swinging round on his heel.

And he set off at cracking pace towards Northbourne Park Villas, the heavy carpet-bag swaying at his side.

Behind him he heard a voice calling softly and cooingly as a pigeon, 'Good luck so.'

In the silent darkness of the big second-floor bedroom at No 53 Mortimer Johnson, lying stiffly on his back in the wide curtained bed, the fine linen sheets and the good woollen blankets weighing on him, abruptly broke a long silence.

'It is no good trusting to luck, my dear,' he said.

He expected his wife to know that he was still speaking about her jewellery. He had warned her about it when, coming in from his dressing-room in nightgown and heavy silk robe, he had found Rosa, her maid, shutting the jewels into the lockfast drawer of the dressing-table and she had failed to go over immediately and turn the key on them. She had taken notice of what he had said to her, of course. But, lying in the dark waiting fruitlessly for sleep, he had been unable to disabuse himself of the idea that when the morning came she would show a similar lack of care.

'No, Mortimer, I understand,' she replied now in the close darkness.

'The very first thing after breakfast you are to take them to the bank. You had better have Burch with you. It is intolerable, quite intolerable, not to have another man-servant in the house. You have spoken to the domestic agency again?'

'Yes, dear. And they promised to send anyone suitable on their books first thing tomorrow.'

'Well, you cannot very well interview them then, can you? Not when you have to be at the bank?'

His irritation frothed up into the dark. But no suggestion followed of any way out of the impasse.

After a while she spoke again.

'Mortimer,' she said, her voice strained with anxiety, 'you do not believe that those horrid men the detective-officers told us of last month will come tonight?'

'I do, my dear,' he said, allowing himself a measure of satisfaction.

She gave a little cry of fear, quickly suppressed.

'But why, Mortimer?' she demanded. 'Why tonight?'

'Because I think they will come every night, my dear. Eternal vigilance is the price of safety.'

The words lingered resoundingly on the hot close air inside the bed-curtains.

Policeman Watson, No 126, was feeling the heat. His heavy serge uniform trousers scraped unpleasantly against the insides of his sweaty thighs at every step. His helmet rested on his brow like a rim of lead. His thick leather belt with its burden of bullseye lantern and heavy wooden alarm-rattle set up its own sticky band of sweat all round his middle. He longed for a drink. A pint of 'XXX' Ale floated like a vision in his thoughts. A pint drawn from a barrel kept in a fine cool cellar.

The notion of it gradually began to prey on his mind till he felt himself, for all the thick darkness of the moonless night, an explorer crossing a vast desert on the point of being driven mad by the heat of the sun.

'I can't go on like this.'

He had actually murmured the words aloud, so oppressive he felt his circumstances to be.

And at that he made up his mind to expel from his brain the sight of that bubble-topped deliciously cool pint, whatever was needed to do so. But there was only one subject that would displace it.

A woman now. A pretty delicate creature like the one he had spoken to just round about here that evening back in the spring. That Rosa. That had been her name, Rosa. Only this one would go on being agreeable. She would not be the sort who would go afterwards with a criminal and flout it in his face. And bother enough there had been about that when he had reported it. But you couldn't have a lady's maid from a house on your beat seen with a notorious cracksman and not say something. You could not.

No, a woman like that Rosa, but different. More biddable, more of a girl. Say one was to come his way just now. Some dollymop of a creature, turned out of a house for being found in the young Master's bed. It happened. It happened all right. So why shouldn't he chance to come across just such a one just now?

And if she had been turned out, there she would be, alone, wanting a friend. Ready to tell her troubles. To tell what she had done. She would have to be punished for that, of course. A girl that would let any young rogue take her into his bed needed a good hid –

The sharp sound of running steps jerked Policeman Watson out of all his reverie. Ahead, some twenty yards along the street, he saw by the light of a distant lamp that someone had come running out of the passageway along there and was heading straight towards him. A girl.

Coster-girl by the look of her, with that short skirt pretty nigh up round her calves. What was she . . . ? No, surely not, not like an answer to his . . . But, yes. Yes, coming straight for him.

'Mr Policeman, Mr Policeman.'

But at the sound of her voice a cold chill descended on him. Irish. You could hear it even in those two words. Irish, and if there was one thing he had learnt in this life it was that you could never trust the Irish. He might take an interest in a girl sometimes, when the opportunity arose on his beat just occasionally, but he had pledged himself that he would never get into the claws of any twisting lying Irish moll.

He looked down at the girl standing in front of him now, panting from her running.

'You're Irish,' he said. 'You're an Irish Cockney.'

'Indeed I am,' she replied, bold as brass. 'A poor Irish girl.'

'Then you'd better go about your business. I know your sort.'

He drew himself up and hooked his thumbs into his belt on either side of his unlit bullseye.

'But – But – ' the girl blabbered. 'But, Mr Policeman, listen. I know I'm Irish, but – But I'm a girl too. An' – An' I need help.'

'It's no duty of a policeman to go giving advice to every sort of ragtag and bobtail,' he declared.

Why couldn't she have been a decent – But never mind that. Perhaps he had deserved this for the thoughts he had been thinking just as the creature came along.

But the creature was not doing as she had been told. Far from going about her business she seemed to be pressing close towards him.

'Please, Mr Policeman. Please, won't yer stop just a minute an' hear what a poor girl's got ter say?'

'I've stopped long enough already. I'm not put on my beat to stand and listen to the likes of you. I'm here to protect the property of respectable people.'

'But can't yer do that just standing here fer a while?'

Impudent hussy.

'I do that by keeping to my patrol. Every street in the beat once in every twenty minutes.'

'But – But if yer stopped just a moment or two, and then went on a bit quicker, like. You'd do it all just as well. An' – An' I'm a girl in great distress, sir.'

The pleading, especially as he could think of no convincing answer, sent a new flush of anger through him. To have all this on top of the heat of the night.

'Be off,' he said. 'Just you be off.'

From what he could make out of her face in the darkness, and he had to admit it was pretty enough face, soft and yielding like enough, she was looking downright perplexed as if she could not think what to do next. Well, there was an answer to that. She could be on her way and leave him alone.

Then, to his total astonishment, the face in front of him abruptly crumpled and a howl of tears rose up into the silent night.

'Stop that,' he blurted out. 'Stop it at once.'

They would be pushing up windows all around in a moment. The gentry would put in complaints. They never liked having their sleep broken.

'Stop it.'

But the howling only grew louder.

'What is it then? What is it?' he demanded, shaking the creature by the shoulder, and conscious as he did so of how soft the flesh was.

With a tremendous gulp she succeeded in stopping the noise.

'Oh, yer will help then? Yer will? I knew yer would. I knew you were a big strong man as a girl could rely on.'

A few more broken sobs came from her.

Well, if she was the sort of girl who wanted a man with a bit of strength to him, a bit of authority, she had come to the right shop. Perhaps too she wasn't so Irish after all. Maybe the father was English and only the mother some Irish slut. And she was young. Young and soft and in need of a firm hand.

'Look, my girl,' he said, 'why don't we step a pace down that passageway there? We don't want all and sundry coming by and seeing you in this sort of a state, do we?'

'Oh no, sir. Thank you, sir.'

And she did what he had suggested. She did it. He thought such things could happen only in his fancy. But with head bent meekly as a lamb's she went in front of him down to the passageway and in at its doubly-dark entrance.

He felt his heart thudding hard under his heavy serge

M

tunic and his mouth was as dry as if he had sucked a lemon.

Lying in her voluminous white nightgown staring upwards, Mrs Mortimer Johnson ventured a word into the thick darkness of the closely curtained bed.

'Dearest, are you awake?'

'What is it now?' came the familiar irritable voice. 'You know very well that on these hot nights I find it difficult to sleep.'

'Yes, dear,' she answered, suppressing at once the idea of pointing out that it had been he who had last broken the silence.

She sighed.

'Would you like some of the lemonade that Cook made?' she asked, half-knowing that she would be snubbed but possessed of a notion that only a cool drink would enable him to get some repose. 'I could ring upstairs for one of the maids.'

'I would like to be left to get to sleep.'

'Yes, dear.'

And she felt constrained to add : 'Good night.'

'Good night.'

But no sooner had final and definitive silence been imposed than it was broken by a sound from outside. It was a sound that to Mrs Johnson's ever-apprehensive ears seemed to come from somewhere appallingly close, the sound of a cat yowling. Three long and curiously distinct separate yowls.

CHAPTER XV

FROM THE SHADOW of the old sycamore tree half-way along Northbourne Park Villas Val and the Manchester Man heard the three cat yowls coming from close by No 53.

'Right, lad, off you go,' whispered the Manchester Man.

Val swallowed once.

'Right,' he answered.

And leaving the Manchester Man deep in the nook between the tree and the wall with at his feet the carpet-bag from which they had taken what he himself would need, he set off at a steady pace towards the house. In his mind he forced himself to repeat over and over again the advice the Manchester Man had given him during their cab journey, 'Take it easy. Never hurry. Wait, and listen.'

He reached the familiar front gate across which he had so often talked to Janey.

Janey, where was she? Safe asleep up at the top of the house with that Maggie? She ought to be. And there ought to be no little round bottle anywhere about in that room of hers now. But would she have used those drops? Ought he to have made her swear that she would?

He lifted the latch on the gate with his fingers so that it did not make the least noise. The sound of their own gate-latch, Noll Sproggs had impressed on him, was something that would wake for an instant all but the heaviest sleepers, leaving them uneasy and watchful.

Slowly he pushed open the gate, alert for the least squeak of the hinges. None came. He stepped through and closed the gate as carefully behind him. 'There's nothing yer crusher notices more nor a gate open,' Noll Sproggs had said.

In the same cautious way he walked the few yards along the path to the foot of the steps. Janey's steps, he thought.

But he pushed that notion out of his mind. He must think of nothing but what he was doing. He mounted the steps.

At the top he stood unmoving for a moment. He knew that he was striving to put off till the last possible instant the first plainly give-away move. If someone unexpectedly came up to the gate behind him now he could still pretend, even if not very convincingly, that he had called by mistake at the wrong house. But after this point he would be marked out beyond any wriggling as an intending thief.

He jerked his gaze away from the brass doorknob, faintly shining.

Over his shoulder he took a quick look back along the street and then another the other way. No one. Nothing.

So Eileen must have met her No 126 all right. She would be at this very moment keeping him somewhere. What was she having to do to hold him? Best not to think. Far and away best not to think. But if only there had been no house at the back with young masters coming home at all hours night after night. If only there had been some way to get into No 53 from the side where a passer-by would not see.

But best to get on with it.

He put one foot up on the low balustrade at the side of the porch, reached forward for the fat black waterspout just beyond and swung himself up. For two seconds he stood with both feet on the flat top of the balustrade, hidden from the street by the broad pillar supporting the front of the porch. Then he reached as high up the waterspout as he could with both hands and at the same time lifted his right foot till it rested on one of the pipe's supports.

And heave up. And reach high again. And scrabble with both feet now. And get a grip with them. And reach high once more. And, yes, the ironwork of the balcony above.

He hauled, scrabbled, kicked out once into the air. And then he was breast-high to the bellying-out balcony railing. And then, the work of a moment, he was over it and standing crouching on the balcony itself.

Had he been noisy? No way of telling.

But what the Manchester Man had said: Take it easy. Never hurry. Wait, and listen.

He flattened himself against the house wall, though against its smooth whiteness he felt he must stand out like a figure at a fairground cockshy. And he waited. The silence of the heavy night came back to him. All he could distinctly hear was the sound of hooves in the far distance, a hansom to judge by the speed. But nothing else seemed to stir. Even the birds, even the insects in the laurel bushes down on either side below, were still, stifled by the heat of the night.

He made himself count up to twenty. And then do it again.

At the end of the second twenty he knew he had to move. A voice in him said stay. He thought of himself as a pillar, there where he was for ever, unnoticed by anyone. But he knew this for a danger, and with a quick shake of his body he moved along the balcony to the window they had fixed on as the best one to go for.

He drew out of his belt the chisel he had taken from the carpet-bag and looked at the window with care. Through the glass he could just make out that, as Janey had told him, the shutters did join in the middle of the window-frame. So, as he had expected, it should be one of the middle panes he should tackle, at the inner corner. He picked on the left-hand one at random and quickly pressed the tip of the chisel blade hard into the very angle of its lower corner.

But the pane seemed firm as a sheet of iron. A new flush of sweat broke out on his forehead and on his stomach.

Don't be a fool, he told himself. You done it more than once as a kid, and using a bit of a chiv only. The old area-diving lay. And most times then the pane didn't give at the first press.

Then, with a single sharp splintering noise that seemed to him up there where anyone could see him like the crack of a whip, the corner of the pane starred.

He plunged down into a crouch.

Wait, and listen. Never hurry. Take it easy.

He waited, not daring even to turn round and look down at the street. At any instant he expected to hear a window somewhere above being pushed sharply up with a jarring rattle and to see some nightgowned figure leaning out with a pistol, ready to fire. To fire into him.

But, no, neither Janey nor Robert had ever said anything about the Master having a pistol. And they had been asked. Noll Sproggs had seen to that.

The night silence, heavy, dusty, smelling of faded flower-scents, horse-dung and his own sweat, swept back into him once more. Slowly he knelt up straight.

Then he set to work on the starred pane. First with the tip of a forefinger pushing one angular piece of glass gently in till it had moved far enough forwards for him to be able to grip the piece next to it between two fingers and work it back and forth. At last it was loose enough to come away, and he laid it carefully on the balcony by his knees. After that it was the work of less than two minutes to remove enough of the long splinters to be able to work on the shutter behind.

From where he had tied it round his chest, he took the shutter-cutter and fitted to it the revolving spike he had put deep into one of his pockets. The tip of the centre spike went into the locked shutter without trouble, though the seasoned wood was harder than the piece he had practised on under Noll Sproggs's tuition. He adjusted the smaller spike so that it would turn within the area of the hole in the pane. His fingers were sweat-covered and slipped on the screw-wheel.

He began to turn the bar. The noise the moving spike made on the wood of the shutter seemed so loud that he could not but feel that it must have woken everybody in the house, the Master and Mistress in their bedroom just one floor above, the butler on his camp-bed in the dining-room a floor below, even Mrs Vickers, Rosa, Maggie and Janey up in their rooms in the attics. Twice he stopped work altogether. But, though he listened hard as he could, he heard nothing and each time he resumed again.

Round and round went the cutting spike, biting deeper at each revolution, at each adjustment of its screw. Round and round, gouging its circular splintered path in the hard wood of the shutter. Then he felt the central spike, pressed against his chest, distinctly move forward as the circle of wood which it was at the middle of gave a little. He turned the bar cautiously for one more full round, and then pressed at the cut circle with his fingertips. It did not yield entirely but it flexed like a slack drum-head. He went back to his cutting for one more round. And then, yes. Yes, he was through.

He pushed gently at the bottom of the circle with his fingers until it gave and he was able to grasp it from the inside. Then he pulled it sharply downwards and, with no more noise than he had been making before, the whole round came clean away.

He pulled it out, laid it down on the balcony beside the shards of broken glass and gave a great sigh.

But he had plenty more to do before he was inside and safely out of view. And there was plenty that could still go wrong even if he escaped the worst, the uncounted-on appearance of Policeman No 126.

He inserted a hand into the hole in the shutter – never hurry – and felt the lining of the heavy curtains within, curiously cool against the backs of his fingers. But he must deal with the catch on the shutters. He manœuvred his hand round about inside and at last he found it. Rapidly he explored it, trying to bring to mind everything Noll Sproggs had told him about the various sorts of catches and how you could tell one from another by touch. It did not take him long to identify this one as a long flat metal bar held in place by a small spring-backed snib. And, yes, there was the snib. And, yes, no difficulty about pressing that home and sliding the bar up over it.

But easy. Easy. A sudden hastiness and the bar might swing right over and come down with a clatter on the far side. And that noise would be right inside the house.

He eased the bar down till it hung pointing straight at the floor. And then he swung the inner half-leaf of the shutter slowly back. It would, he knew, be pushing the curtain behind it outwards a little. If there was anyone in the room behind, the drawing-room as they called it, they would see. But there ought not to be a soul there, certainly not anyone sitting in the dark.

Now, with the shutter moved back, he was able to reach up to the catch of the window. It was just possible to see his hand through the glass and to make out what kind of a catch he had to deal with. Clicking it softly back hardly took a moment.

And, once again, wait. Wait, and listen.

Nothing. The house slept on in the sticky heat. Behind, the street with all the other houses in it was too lapped in thick silence.

Gently push the bottom frame of the window up. Slowly, slowly. Many a window rattled and creaked like billy-oh when it was opened. So, slowly.

But at length the frame was up high enough for him to be able to get himself through. He pushed the shutter behind further back, dragging the heavy curtain a little open as he did so. Still no sound from the street below. Above all, not the steady pacing of the patrolling peeler. So, now to go in.

He crawled over the low sill, felt thick carpet under his outstretched hands, was surprised by it for a moment until he recollected what Janey had told him of her visit to this drawing-room. There was a smell, too, that was unexpected as he brought the rest of his body into the room. He snuffed at it. Yes, beeswax from the furniture they polished every day. And roses. There must be a vase of them somewhere about. And the lingering traces of a woman's scent. It all added up to money, to a life far removed from anything he had ever got near. But that wouldn't be so long in righting itself.

He got to his feet. He must not forget he had work to do.

He turned back in the thick velvety darkness of the room and felt with his hands till he had located the shutter. Then he quietly closed it and made sure that the thick curtains had fallen into place in front of it. The wood of the shutter was painted, if what Robert had told them was correct, a dark brown. Close up against the window it would make the hole in the left-hand middle pane invisible. No need for the messy job of pasting dark paper on it.

He swivelled round until he was facing into the pitchy-black room again, took from the pocket in which he had put his heavy life-preserver one of the three silent lights that the Manchester Man had allowed him and struck it against his lifted boot-heel.

In the little flare of orange light he was able to make out something of the big heavily-furnished room. That must be the piano Janey had told him about. And there was the table with the heavy green cloth over it. And there were chairs up against the wall on the far side and a glass-fronted cabinet. Robert had said the things in that were worth having, and later they would have them. But for the present the thing was to get across to the door as quickly as possible and without bumping into any of the armchairs set here, there and everywhere. No time to linger.

While the tiny flame still burnt he made his way on tiptoe over to the tall mahogany door and tried the knob. As he had expected from what Janey had told him, the door was locked.

Curling-tongs now. He slipped them from his other pocket and had time to kneel and get their tips into the keyhole before the match held between the fingers of his left hand burnt so low that he had to flick it out.

He decided to work on the key on the far side of the door without striking another light. He might well need both the remaining two before he had done his share in here. He slid the tongs further into the keyhole. And, yes, as Robert had told them, the key had been left in. So no need for noisy jemmying open of the heavy door. He eased the long jaws of the tongs slightly apart and tried to push them forward again. With difficulty he advanced them a quarter of an inch or so. He clasped them tight then and started to turn them. But he sensed at once that they were going round without gripping the shaft of the key on the far side. Hoping against hope he went on slowly turning. But when he had got round a whole half-circle he had to admit that the key had not budged. There had been no satisfying click of the tongue of the lock shooting back.

Would there ever be? Was the trick going to work? Noll Sproggs had said it always did, unless the lock was very old or stiff. 'An' that's a nice new 'ouse as yer going into, lad. An' one where things is done proper. Locksmith visits once a year I make no doubt. You'll be all right.' But he wasn't all right. He wouldn't be. He'd have to break the door open after all. And the noise that would make. He'd be bound to wake someone. The butler with his gun. The Master. Someone.

Steady, steady, he said to himself. Try it again. Be patient.

He wiped his hands on the tail of his coat, took a deep breath and pushed at the tongs to see if he could get them a little bit further in. He thought at last that he had felt a small movement. But would it be enough?

Gripping the tongs with all the force of both his hands, he began to turn them, bringing the whole weight of his body to the action. And surely this felt different from the time before? He gripped like a demon and heaved himself half over striving to turn the tongs.

And then, beautifully sweet to his ear, came the soft click of a well-cared-for lock shooting back.

All the tension slid out of his body and he knelt with his forehead against the polish-smelling wood of the door, breathing as hard as if he had run a mile. Then slowly he pulled the tongs out, replaced them carefully in his pocket and got to his feet. He tried the handle of the door. It opened easily and silently.

Outside on the landing he stood breathing as quietly as he could and listening. Wait, and listen.

But there was nothing. Not a single sound of any kind came from the sleeping and thick-muffled house.

He took the second silent light from his pocket, lifted his foot and struck the match against his heel again. The sound of it igniting was so slight that he hardly heard it himself.

By the small circle of light that sprang up he was able to see the stairs ahead of him, the heavily-carved newel-post at the corner of them, the thick red stair-carpet, even the gleam of the brass stair-rods.

Quickly, while the light still lasted, he set out down. It was only when he was half-way that he remembered that Noll Sproggs had told him he must keep well to the side, 'just on the edge o' the carpet, lad, just on the edge.' Had he made any noise? He could have sworn that he had not. The boards under him had been solid and uncreaking as stone.

But the pause he had made when the thought had struck him and the extra care he had taken as he had begun going down again had used up precious time. Just at the turn on to the last flight down to the hall his match went out.

He stood a little while in the darker-seeming darkness and thought. And at last he decided to risk making the rest of the journey down without light. He had had a glimpse of the stairs ahead and felt sure there were no obstacles in his way. He put a hand on the fat banister rail, smooth and polished under his touch, and began going cautiously on downwards.

At last his exploring foot encountered not another step down but the floor of the hall. Now he knew he had to light his third and final match. He could not be sure of getting across to the front door in silence without it. But what if the lock and bolts on that turned out to be more difficult to open than they had expected? Both Janey and Robert had told him how they were arranged. But it was not always easy to be sure from someone else's bare words what a thing looked like.

But risk it. The only way.

Again the match struck with scarcely a sound. The hall sprang to life by its light. He made his way across it as fast as he dared. One of those shut doors, the one on the right of course, was the dining-room. Behind it that butler would be sleeping on his camp-bed. A sound might wake him. But he had to hurry.

The little flame of the match tapered sharply backwards with the speed of his progress. He slowed himself up. If it went out now . . .

But the flame steadied itself and a couple of moments later he had reached the door. Yes, long bolts top and bottom. No difficulty there, only making sure to draw them slowly and silently. And, yes, best of all, the key in the lock as Robert had sworn it always was. And the chain.

No trouble there either.

He set to work, first to turn the key so as not to let it snick too loudly, then to pull back one after the other top bolt and bottom, and finally to unhook the chain making sure it did not rattle. The silent light in his left hand went out just as he had finished lowering the chain. But no matter. He needed no light now.

Smiling to himself for the first time in all that evening, quietly and slowly he drew open the big front door.

CHAPTER XVI

IN THE CLOSE darkness of the narrow cul-de-sac passage-way not much more than five minutes' walk from Northbourne Park Villas, with only a thin strip of faintly lighter grey cloud-obscured sky above, Eileen moved sharply away from the groping hands of Policeman Watson, No 126.

' 'Ere, Mr Policeman, watch what yer a-doing.'

Surely she had kept him here nearly long enough now. She could afford to put herself at the edge of his reach.

Policeman Watson answered thickly.

'Now, don't you come that with me, my lass. I know girls o' your sort. This ain't the first time by many a mile you been close up to a man.'

His voice in the darkness rose higher with every word. Eileen noted the wildness and the weakness. They indicated danger. But, she thought, she would not need to let him get too close again.

She retreated half a pace when he took a hasty and uncertain step towards her.

'You're all the same,' he complained. 'First you want it, then all on a sudden you don't want anything to do with it. All o' you. Miss Butter-wouldn't-melt from No 53, her and her cracksman. You're all the same.'

But two words among all the sudden incoherent diatribe had struck Eileen with unexpected force. She felt a sharp stirring of irrational curiosity. 'No 53'. The very house number that had been at the back of her mind for every second that she had coaxed and tricked Policeman Watson into staying here with her a minute or two more. That number coupled with his muttered mention of a 'cracksman'. What could it mean?

It seemed plain to her that the 'all o' you' he kept coming back to was much more likely to be 'one o' you'. From everything that he had said so far she knew that he was no sure-of-himself ram, not for all his talk of 'knowing what a girl wants and where'. But this one girl who had so upset him, this one from No 53, why should it be a girl from No 53 Northbourne Park Villas?

Yet something told her that it was.

She decided to go a little nearer him, though she kept a careful watch on the white blurs that were hands.

'An' – An' what's that about Butter-wouldn't-melt?' she asked, infusing her voice with tremendous coyness.

'Ah, caught her out all right. But never mind that one. It's you we're a-considering. You and your wicked ways.'

He reached out with an unexpected swift lunge and caught her by the wrist. Trapped, she thought. You silly fool. What if . . .

But her instinctive tugging immediately revealed that in his sweat-slippery grasp there was no danger. She let her arm go slack.

'I bet you've caught out a good many in your time, Mr Policeman,' she said.

'Dare say I have.'

A pause, no doubt for courage gathering. She could hear his breath in the hot darkness.

'And I knows what to do with 'em when I've caught 'em.'

'A big man like you,' she risked saying. And then she

quickly added: 'But tell us about your Miss Butter-wouldn't-melt.'

'No better than she should be. I seen 'em. Seen 'em at it. But it's you we're a-dealing with just now.'

Them. At it? At it?

She turned a little away.

'No, go on,' she said. 'I want to know about that.'

His answer was a little long in coming, but came thumpingly.

'Who's a Curiosity Cat then? A naughty little Curiosity Cat?'

'Sure an' it's meself. But you must satisfy that curiosity o' mine. Before anything.'

It was playing with fire to have added those last words, and she knew it. But his ponderous turning of the talk back and back to his own particular wishes somehow made her all the more certain that Miss Butter-wouldn't-melt could only be the girl from No 53 Northbourne Park Villas. Val's girl, Janey, the Janey he had once sworn was to her 'no more than the butt-end of a candle beside the biggest gas-chandelier o' them all.'

Again Policeman Watson was silent, breathing like a rhinoceros in the darkness. She thrust her face a little nearer to his. And it worked.

'Satisfy that curiosity before?' he said. 'All right then, we will. She was a maid-servant from a house round about here as I happened to get acquainted with.'

'From No 53?'

'Yes, that's about the size of it. And now – '

'But which street? Which street?'

'Ain't it a Curiosity now?'

'Oh, I am, I am. But tell me.'

'No harm in telling, I suppose. She's from No 53 North-bourne Park Villas, only a step from – '

Eileen was unable to stop herself gasping aloud, half at the absolute confirmation of her suspicion, half in a rush of pure hate at the thought of her Val and that girl 'at it', as this blowing puffing brute had said.

'Now then, what's all this to you?' Policeman Watson asked, plainly surprised at the violence of her reaction.

'Nothing, nothing,' she answered hastily, hardly able to take in what he was saying so boilingly was she alive with inner rage.

'So,' came the heavy distant voice, 'now we've satisfied that curiosity we'll have to think about paying for it.'

'Oh,' she burst out in total exasperation.

And, wrenching her wrist from his sweaty paw, she turned and ran hard as she could up to the top of the passageway and out into the night, her mind a bubbling cauldron of white fury.

Janey lay on her lumpy mattress, still awake. She felt sticky in every least part of her body down to her sweat-slithery toes. The low-ceilinged room right under the roof, which the sun had been baking till the low thunder-clouds had come rolling up towards evening, was insufferably hot.

'Maggie?' she whispered into the darkness. 'Maggie? You awake?'

There was no answer. Maggie's thick breathing continued on the same droning note.

At least she's out of it. But was there really something to be out of? Were they really coming soon? Were they here already, prowling about in the house below? Thank God I did give those drops to Mr Burch.

Or will those be making him bad? Is he lying there in

the dining-room in a dead faint? Or dying, even dying? No. No, that can't happen. Armstrong's Black Drops is taken regular. They can't do him no harm.

She heaved herself on to her side in the narrow bed. Its clumps of pressed-hard flock seemed even harder to-night. No way to keep clear of them.

God, I wish I knew what was happening. I wish I knew if they really are coming. If they're here. If they're here.

As soon as the Manchester Man had entered the house he had set down the heavy carpet-bag and pushed the door closed behind him. Val remembered him saying in the cab that it was as needful to have a door unlocked ready to get out of in a hurry as it was to have it looking well shut from the outside. Then he sharply ordered him to take off his boots. This was something he had forgotten amid all the instructions and advice.

He stooped quickly and untied the laces.

'An' put 'em where you can pick 'em up easy if we're misfortunate,' the Manchester Man whispered sharply. 'There's been more than one lad traced by his gallies.'

Val placed the boots with care just by the door.

'Where to then?' he whispered, as he stood up.

'Masks on and then the plate-closet. If what we learnt about that door's only half true, we've work enough there. But first you go an' make sure as that butler's sound away. I mistrust that blower o' yours an' them drops.'

'She'll have used 'em,' Val whispered in quick defence of Janey.

But, slipping on his clinging mask, he went speedily as he could across to the dining-room door.

Yet, kneeling there with his ear to the keyhole, he heard at once deep and reverberant snores. He signed to the

Manchester Man, who was busy lighting the dark lantern, that it was all right.

'Go in,' came the harsh whispered reply.

For a moment he rebelled. To go into a room where a man was on guard, though asleep. Where he had a loaded shotgun beside him.

But the Manchester Man was not a person to disobey. Val rose and slowly turned the doorknob. It moved with blessed silentness. He eased the door open. With eyes by now well accustomed to the dark he was able to make out by the faint light coming through the door behind him the big table running the length of the room. He took a step forward and then directed his gaze towards the sound of the heavy snoring. After a little he thought he could see where the bed was.

Step by slithering step he approached it. There was never the least change in the butler's drugged breathing. At last he was only a yard away. He took a short step nearer and leant forward to see what he could of the butler's face. And his bare toes just touched the shotgun he had been unable to see on the floor. It tipped to its side with a clatter that seemed louder than a cascade of falling tinware.

But the snoring continued as if there had not been the least sound.

Val forced himself forward again from where he had jumped back. He stooped and located the gun. Carefully he picked it up and crept back with it into the hall. In triumph he held it in the thin ray of light coming from the dark-lantern.

'Get a bit o' rope across from the door to the newel-post,' came the hard voice in reply.

Black with resentment, he did as he had been told.

When he had finished he found that the Manchester Man had gone into the breakfast-room. He followed him in. The dark-lantern had been set on the sideboard, on a dish from which the Manchester Man had tumbled a pile of oranges. Its rod-thin ray was playing directly on the door of the plate-closet, from which the heavy screen had been carelessly pushed aside.

At last, Val thought.

The Manchester Man paid him not the least notice. He was busy setting up the peter-cutter, fixing in the first of the bits. When it was ready, still without a word, he approached the iron door of the closet, thrust the base pivot of the cutter into the keyhole and swung his full weight on the other end to get maximum leverage. Then, with this great force behind the bit, he began to heave it round.

Val stood and watched. After five minutes or less he was surprised when the Manchester Man broke off, looked over at him and said tersely : 'Your turn, lad.'

But when he came to the work himself he understood at once why five minutes at a time was enough. Unless he kept his full strength bearing down so as to lever the bit hard against the iron of the door it simply slipped round uselessly. It was all he could do to master the knack during his first spell at it, and he was never so relieved as when at last he heard the Manchester Man's hard voice behind him saying 'Give it me.'

So for five-minute spell after five-minute spell they took it in turns. After he had had four attempts, Val found he was able to make as much progress during his stints as the Manchester Man. But for both of them it seemed precious little. And he reckoned they would have to make at least six holes before there was any chance of wrenching out the lock.

During one of his spells at work he noticed suddenly the strong smell of oranges and when he had finished he found that the Manchester Man had been fiercely chewing one of the fruit from the spilled dish. He took another himself. With the heat of the night and the labour of drilling he was thirsty as a mule.

Spell after spell went by. One by one they ground out the holes round the lock. Val lost count of time. He lost count of the number of oranges he had eaten. And still the lock in the iron door seemed firm as ever.

But it was during one of Val's turns at the cutter that he felt a sudden thrust forward and the whole tool lurched inwards. It came as such a surprise he was unable to stop himself giving a little cry of alarm.

'Ssssh, you fool,' came the Manchester Man's harsh whisper. 'Stay quiet. And listen.'

Val stood rooted to the spot in front of the door. After a little his ears began to acknowledge the tiny sounds all round him, the Manchester Man's breathing, still fast from his last spell at the cutter, a faint metallic pinging once or twice from the hot dark-lantern, the distant barking of a dog and, louder, the sound of St Stephen's Church clock striking three.

But there was nothing else, and at last the Manchester Man moved. He went over to the closet door, carefully adjusted the peter-cutter and threw his full weight into levering it upwards. And the weakened lock gave. There was one rending squeak, a sharp 'Ah' from the Manchester Man, and then Val saw the lock that had defied them so long being slowly prised out.

And then it was free and the Manchester Man quietly swung the door wide. Val stepped quickly forward. The little beam of the dark-lantern scarcely reached into the deep interior of the shelved cupboard. But it neverthe-less caught and reflected glint after glint from silver object after silver object ranged round it high and low.

Wealth. It was wealth. It was a ladder lowered from above into the pit of his life and up it he could climb and start afresh in the daylight. There in front of him was release from the prison he had been in since the day he was born. And he had driven his way to it.

In the heavy double-darkness of the curtained bed Mrs Mortimer Johnson, conscious of the hours she had lain awake, her mind a long chronicle of little mysterious unaccounted-for sounds, missing the familiar satisfied snoring of the father of her children, ventured to speak.

'Mortimer, are you awake?'

There was a long pause before a reply came.

'I thought you were sleeping.'

'No,' she said. 'No, I pretended to be so in order not to keep you wakeful.'

'And I the same,' he replied, in that resignedly melan-choly tone she so seldom heard, and which when she heard she treasured.

He sighed.

'It's very late, my dear,' he said. 'St Stephen's clock has struck three.'

'I heard. You cannot get to sleep?'

She put the scarcely logical question without thinking. At almost all other times it would have received a scathing answer. But now the reply was questing and troubled.

'I am anxious. Anxious about the house. Anxious about young Frederick. Anxious about the servants. It weighs on me all. What if some violent and desperate men were to break in? They might. It's well known we're people of substance. Why, the jewels in that lockfast are worth almost two thousand.'

By day, in any other circumstances, he would have said 'well over two thousand.' But, lying not touching him in the broad bed, she hardly let the thought surface to the very back of her mind.

'But, dear,' she answered softly, 'we have taken every precaution. You know we have.'

'I hope I have done my duty,' he answered with a passing return of his daylight self. 'But what about the servants? You cannot always guard against human fallibility.'

'But why should men like that come here?' she asked, her voice a plaintive demand in the darkness. 'There are other houses, next door, at the back. And they are every bit as vulnerable as ourselves. Why should they choose No 53?'

'You're good to me, my dear,' he said, extending his hand till it found hers and for a moment clasped it. 'You're good to me. But they might. They might.'

'Then you must reflect,' she said, jutting her chin up above the heavy smoothness of the sheet, 'that you have done everything that duty could to protect us.'

The little defiance hovered between them in the stifling air. And after a while he spoke again.

'Thank you for saying that, my dear. I think perhaps I shall sleep now.'

'I'm sure you will. We can both sleep now. Everything possible has been done to safeguard all here.'

And before a whole minute had passed the hot enclosed box of the curtained bed was at last murmurous with two sleepers' calm and regular breathing.

CHAPTER XVII

It was as if victory in the assault on the plate-closet door had released a devil in them. A joint devil that gripped not only Val himself but the Manchester Man, for all that Val never once saw him smile in any chance ray of the dark-lantern nor did he ever utter even the briefest and quietest of laughs. But plainly he was possessed of the same ransacking fire that Val had felt burn in him from the moment he set his hands on the ranks and rows of silver in the closet.

They bundled the store of plate into their sacks with an abandon at complete variance with their utter caution before. In the closeness of the big cupboard they let centre-piece and candelabra clang together careless of the sound.

And, when the deep shelves had been emptied to the last piece, and two bulging sacks had been placed beside the hall door ready for the moment that Old Henry's cat-yowl all-safe signal would come, they began to roam and range together through all the uninhabited lower part of the house. Each carrying a capacious oat-smelling sack, they seized anything and everything that happened to catch their fancy, vases, inkwells, paper-weights, trinket boxes, the entire contents of the glass-fronted cabinet in the drawing-room without so much as one assessing glance, knick-knacks, small pictures off the walls, photographs in their frames, the locked tantalus from the library, the heavy gilt drawing-room clock from under its glass dome. When they went down to the basement the Manchester Man began to plunder the servants' boxes as eagerly as he had looted bureau and table up above. For a moment the sight of him flinging out the boxes' contents, the brushes and the dusters, the pots of this and jars of that, made Val come to a halt. For a moment, thinking that the box at that instant being despoiled looked very like Janey's, seen so often on the house steps, he wanted to protest. But almost at once the spirit of rapine flowed back into him.

And besides, he told himself, it'd look damned peculiar if her box was the only one to be left untouched.

So he joined in once more, and even had the vengeful satisfaction of doing what Climbing Charlie had once boasted to him that he would like to do, 'to prig that old Cookie's savings.'

The rampage, fierce though it was, did not last long however. Not much more than a quarter of an hour sufficed to denude first floor, ground floor and basement of every portable object of the least value. And then, when it came to moving on up the stairs to the floors where the bedrooms were, all the Manchester Man's iron-hard caution came back with a rush.

He laid a hand on Val's arm. The grip was fierce as a clamp.

'Go quiet, lad. Nobody told us owt about pistols, but if the Master do have a pair somewhere close by him he won't be the first.'

The word 'pistols' was all that was needed in Val's mind. It came like a shock of water flung from an ice-rimmed pail. For the second time since he had begun the break-in he thought of himself receiving a bullet in the body, of gouged-apart flesh and smashed bone. He almost backed away down the stairs. But the Manchester Man, toweringly tall, black-masked, was behind him.

'See if they're snoring, first of all,' he whispered. 'You take the attics and the top floor, I'll have the second floor where the Master is.'

Together they crept up the stairs. Val, armed with a taper, decided to go right up to the top to begin with. Janey would be there. With his ear close to the door of her room, matchboard that rather than thick mahogany, he would be able to hear her breathing and Maggie's too no doubt. He would silently wish her good luck, standing there so close to her. Poor kid, she would need luck in the days ahead. She had been good to him. If it hadn't been for the chance of his meeting Eileen, things might have been different.

To be so close to her. Perhaps if he was sure both of them were sleeping deeply he would open the door, take a look at her. That hair of hers on the pillow. A parting look.

Perhaps he would.

Softly the Manchester Man closed behind him the door of the bedroom where he had left Master and Mistress soundly sleeping behind the curtains of the big bed. He pocketed the set of betties which had just well proved its worth on the lockfast. Then he set the dark-lantern down on the floor, carefully placing it close to the banister where there was no carpet for it to singe – nothing more likely to wake folk than the smell of burning – and in its small spot of light knelt to examine his haul.

Why, he thought as the necklaces and the brooches, the lockets and the bracelets, the ear-rings and the pendants poured out in a soft sparkling heap on the carpet, why there must be two thousands worth. Two thousand. Aye, and here's a ring as'll do for meself. That lad's a fool.

He slipped into one of his waistcoat pockets an emerald ring whose jewel had glinted large and green in the thin beam of light.

And, as he looked up to do so, he realized, with a slow gradualness that was like morning mist drifting away from an unfamiliar landscape, that he was looking at a person standing on the lowest stair of the flight that led to the top of the house. It was a skirt he saw first, a black skirt at the edge of the lantern ray. And then, as slowly and incredulously he raised his eyes still further, he made out the cramped black bodice, seemingly put on in haste and awry, and at last a pinched and elderly face.

And it was no one who should have been there.

The thought boomed in his head. They had gone over and over the folk of the house. That was the way. To have each one of them in your mind, so that if one did rise from their bed you knew at once who they were and had a good notion of how best to take them. But there should not have been any old lady. This could not be the cook, young Val had described her well. This person just should not be there.

'Then who are you?'

He spoke the words aloud, almost loud enough to have woken the sleepers in the room behind him had it not been for the stoutness of the mahogany door.

'I am the governess in this establishment. And I do not need to ask who you are. I have been awake a long time hearing small unaccountable noises. And at last I knew that I had to come out.'

'You'd ha' done better to keep your head under the blanket,' he answered, guessing now that she slept on the floor above and that that young fool had begun by going right to the attics.

'I wished to stay where I was,' she answered. 'But I had my young charge to consider.'

'Charge?'

And only then did what it meant her calling herself 'Governess of this establishment' sink fully in. Governess meant a kid, her charge. Why hadn't they known there was a kid in the house? Had they been tricked all along by that dollymop of Val's? What sort of a kid was it? Would it wake at any moment and start howling? What had gone wrong? Why had all their talk with the footman not hit on this?

The questions poured into his mind.

He snatched up the dark-lantern, careless of its heat on his fingers, and rose to his feet pointing its beam at the figure on the stairs.

'Don't come near me.'

He stopped just where he was. There had been an assurance in the words that went ill with the person he had thought he was faced with. They had been no frightened plea.

'Don't come a step nearer,' she repeated. 'I have a water flask in my hand, held over the banisters. If I drop it, it will waken Mr Johnson instantly. And he sleeps with a loaded pistol hidden in the cabinet beside him.'

The devil he does, he thought. I should have opened that cabinet. Only it was so close to the bed.

He drew in a sharp breath through his nostrils. He must do something quickly. She had not tried to wake the house as she should have done. He must try to take advantage of that.

'Missus,' he said, speaking low and quickly, saying something, anything, so as to continue keeping her quiet.

'Well?'

His rapid thoughts seized on a half-grasped idea.

'Missus, will you listen to what I've got to say?'

'I ought to call out to Mr Johnson.'

He knew he had got her with that. If she kept to saying and not doing, she would stay quiet for a little. But he must use that little to the full.

Where the devil was the lad Val?

'No, missus,' he said. 'Don't you call out. Wait till you've heard my side.'

'Your side? You cannot have a side. You are in a gentleman's house, flagrantly caught.'

'Aye,' he said rapidly. 'Aye, I'll not deny I came here to rob.'

'Then –'

He cut in quickly.

'No, listen. I was here to rob, but to rob the place. To rob him, the Master. Not the governess. I know about governesses. I've heard on the life they they live, a dog's life.'

'You must not say that,' she shot out.

Ha, he thought, that went home then. I'll keep on this way.

'Oh, I mustn't say it, eh? But it's the truth, aren't it? An' we're told we mun speak truth.'

'But – but –'

He savoured her dilemma. Keep her like this and she would soon be eating out of his hand.

'But,' she managed to get out at last, 'there are times when in speaking the truth we should exercise a proper discretion.'

'I know nowt about that,' he said sharply. 'All I know is what's so. You're governess here, and they make your life a rare misery. That's so, aren't it? That's the truth, an' shame the devil.'

'I will acknowledge that my life is not always easy.'

She was running. Keep her so.

'Ah, I knew you'd come to it. I knew you'd see it my way.'

'Your way?' she said unexpectedly. 'I could hardly do that. There is a great difference in our stations.'

'Oh no, there's not,' he answered quickly and hard. 'Not half so much as you'd like to think. Nay, not a quarter. Oh, aye, I'm poor to starving and I was setting that right by thieving. But you. What different case are you in?'

'A very different one, I assure you.'

'Oh ho, are you rich then?' he scoffed.

'A gentlewoman,' she replied, with a little access of dignity, 'need never be ashamed of admitting to poverty. If that state is undeserved.'

'So he pays you precious little,' he answered with brutality.

'He?'

'Why, him asleep in there, your master.'

'I am not a servant.'

He laughed, softly and jeeringly.

'And he treats you as if you were different from a servant?' he asked.

He hoped fiercely that his shot had gone home. It should have done, if all he had heard about governesses was true.

And she was hesitating to answer. But where the hell was that lad?

'I refuse to listen to questions of that sort.'

Up on her high horse. He had struck home, by God. 'No,' he said rapidly. 'You dare not listen.'

'I choose not to.'

'Pooh,' he said, 'you can choose nowt else. He pays you nobbut a pittance, and he treats you downright bad. There's no way round that. And it puts you fair and square on my side o' the fence.'

He hammered home the last words, all but certain of her now.

And it looked as though he was going to be proved right.

She came down off the step above him, though he saw that she still held the water flask over the banister rail.

'And you wish me,' she said, in a quiet clear voice, 'to act in confederation with you? To leave you to carry out what you came here to do?'

'Aye, missus,' he answered. 'You've seen it. What d'you owe him? Let him sup bitter medicine for once. He's seen you take many a draught, I warrant.'

'Yes. He has.'

'That's the right on it then,' he said with brusque reassurance. 'Now get you back to that bed o' yourn and put your head under the covers till morning.'

He laughed.

'Aye, and then you'll have a rare sight to see.'

'But I am not going to go.'

He almost backed away so suddenly cold and determined were the words.

'Not?'

It was the most he could manage to say.

'No,' she said. 'You see, you have not taken into account that I have a duty.'

'Duty? What duty?'

He wished he could get the hang of it again. He was sure he had talked his way right out of it. And it seemed now that he had been getting nowhere at all.

And where was the lad?

'I could not expect a person of your sort to understand. But it is my duty to safeguard the rights of my employer, however it should happen that he treats me. And you are violating those rights. So it is my duty to call to him.'

'No,' he said, putting all the force he could into it while keeping his voice low enough not to penetrate that thick door.

He longed to use other means to keep the old hag quiet, to slip the eel-skin from his pocket and silence her with a single blow. But she had raised that damned water-bottle high, as if she guessed what would come into his mind.

'Yes,' she countered. 'Yes, it is my duty to call him.'

'No. Hear me. You've heard me up to this. Hear me a little more.'

Would it work? It was usually a good bet to play on their feeling for what was fair. But . . .

'Well, I have heard you. And I will hear you. But I must warn you I still know what my duty is. And I will still hold this flask over the banister.'

'Oh, aye,' he answered, hope beginning to beat again within him. 'Hold it there all you want. Hold it till doomsday. It won't make a ha'porth o' difference. There's no necessity.'

'Nevertheless,' she replied, with a quaver in her voice, 'I shall continue to hold it.'

'There's no necessity,' he went on, more and more hopeful with every second that she failed to raise the alarm, 'because you're right about what you said o' me.'

'What I said of you?'

'Aye,' he answered, infusing sadness into his voice. 'Aye, I thought I could trick you. I thought I could. But what I never came near knowing was that you had what you said you had.'

'A sense of duty,' she replied, with wonder.

'Aye, just that. But, you see, I never stood a chance of having any o' that myself. I were brought up where they'd never heard on it.'

'But surely . . .'

'No. You never could have an idea o' the way I were brought up, of the life I lived as a child. Child? It were more like an animal.'

He felt confident that he was laying it on not a bit too thickly. And her answer confirmed his belief.

'I see. You had no knowledge of religion? Of God? Of Our Saviour?'

'Not till I was full growed. And, oh, missus, it were too late then. Too late till now.'

'Now?'

He caught the palpitating interest in her tone. Hooked again, by God. And better this time.

'Yes,' he said. 'Too late till now. But, missus, look at these.'

He stooped and picked up the jewellery that had lain on the carpet unregarded.

'Look,' he said, 'I'll put it all in your keeping. Every last blessed bit.'

He moved towards her with it.

'Keep back,' she said at once.

He halted, afraid that after all his fish was free. But it seemed he had no need to fear.

'You may put them down just where you are,' she said. 'And then go back.'

He did as she had asked with every sign of penitence that he could muster.

'But why?' she asked, as he slowly stood up again. 'Why?'

'Because I've finished, missus. Finished with the thieving lay now and for ever. Along o' you.'

'Of me?'

'Aye, of you. Little frail old lady as you are, you've downed the Manchester Man. Summat as no peeler, no pair o' peelers, nay no three on 'em has done yet.'

And, with all the drama he could rise to, he tore the crude black-cotton mask from his face.

'But I don't understand,' she said.

'From this out,' he repeated, 'I've given up thieving. Given it up to the last drop.'

'Can I believe that?'

If you do, he thought grimly, you'll believe anything. But he made his face as hang-dog as he knew how.

'You must believe it, missus. You must.'

She stood there in the faint light from the dark-lantern, weighing him up. And at last she spoke.

'Yes, I believe you.'

'I knowed it,' he said, letting relief pour into the words, a relief that was not a little true.

'But –'

He jerked his head up at her tone.

'But I must add this : I cannot let you go.'

Rage came choking back into him.

'You cannot –'

'No,' she said, in the clear explanatory voice he had already found maddening enough. 'No, you may repent, but you have still done wrong. And it is my duty –'

And at that merciful moment he saw the sudden shadow of the lad behind her on the stairs. The arm holding the water-bottle was swiftly smothered to her side. A soft eel-skin descended soundlessly.

CHAPTER XVIII

STANDING LEANING heavily forwards down the stairs with at his feet the sprawled black-dressed form of the governess, looking so shrunken as to be not much larger than a big doll, Val heard at this moment, clearly penetrating the thick silence, the sound of a cat yowling. Once, twice, three times. He saw the Manchester Man look up, sudden fierce delight glowing on his sombre black-moustached face.

To both Mr and Mrs Mortimer Johnson, deep in sleep inside the stiff curtaining of their big bed, the sound of three cat yowls came distantly and distortedly. More than once since sleep had at last visited them noises that should not have been, for all that they had not been loud, had almost reached through the swathing layers of their dreams. Now the sharp clear cat-calls penetrated equally to each of them, eerily echoing the exactly similar sound they had heard much earlier in the hot night. Both rose fully to consciousness. But both of them were too exhausted to stay awake for more than a few instants. The smoky coils writhed up once more and claimed them.

To Janey, tossing on her narrow lumpy mattress, unsure whether she was asleep or awake, a clear out-of-nowhere cat-sound only added to the confused state of puzzlement she had been experiencing for she did not know how long. It had taken her hours to get to sleep: that she knew. But she thought that she had been asleep at least for some part of the night. Then had she woken? Lying flat on her back with that all too familiar particularly hard little lump of flock poking like an irritated finger into the lower part of her left shoulder-blade, had she really seen, through her almost closed eyes, the door of the room slowly opening inch by inch? And had it really been Val, that mysterious black-masked figure that had seemed to stand there for so long looking down at her? It had had the shape of Val she was sure, that shape she could conjure up in her mind's eye whenever she wanted. But had that been all she had been doing? Letting herself see her own picture of him?

Had she dreamt him? Or had she seen him? And why had that cat yowled in such a funny way twice in one night? Once early on and now again when it must be nearly dawn?

She turned on her side and tried to scrape a few minutes' more sleep from the worn remains of the hot night.

The sound of Old Henry's all-clear signal, the victory trumpet calling loud and clear above the diminishing noise of battle, came to Eileen's ears like a jab of spiteful frustration.

'Hurry,' she shouted to the policemen on either side of her. 'Hurry, or they'll get away.'

She was all fire. At some time, she did not know when, in a night of torment and rage, a night of storming through the deserted lamplit streets heedless of where she went or what happened to her, she had plunged for fire. Had it been too late a time? There was no room in her now for anything but a consuming desire to find that it had not. She had plunged for fire, and now burn it must. Burn who it would, let it burn.

From the moment that, encouraging and avoiding Policeman Watson in that narrow passageway, she had discovered that Val, her Val, had been feeding her on lies, that he had been loving that dollymop, the rage had run in her. At first it had done no more than drive her away from that place. It had been pure luck that she had run out of it even, and not down the passage to the locked wooden gate into the garden of the big house in the next street. But she had run out and turned the first way that she had seen. Luck again that her wild clattering flight had not taken her near Northbourne Park Villas. There the ever watchful Old Henry would without doubt at the sight of her have let out into the night air the sharp and urgent whine of a bitch on heat signalling 'Danger, danger' and sending Val and the Manchester Man dodging and running into safety.

There had been moments in her night-long roaming of the streets when she had almost convinced herself that Val could not have done what she thought he had, when all she had known of him in the months they had lived together seemed to deny that it could be so. There had been times when, though she knew he had betrayed her, she believed she could love him still. Sometimes she had even tried to convince herself that she had been mistaken in what she had heard in the passageway.

But how could there have been a mistake, she had asked herself in the end every time. Policeman Watson had seen Val. Why should he make up a tale about that for her, a chance-met girl? What he had said had to be true, the words had been forced out of him by feelings coming up from the very depths. No, Val had been with that girl. Val had been with Janey. Janey was the gas-chandelier and herself no more than the guttering butt-end of a candle.

Then the rage had run hither and thither in her like black snakes of fire. And at last it had won.

At last it had driven her, a coster-girl all her life, one of a tribe the peelers best loved to persecute, to go to the police. It had driven her to stride through the streets till she had found another policeman than her Watson, No 126, clunkingly pounding his beat. It had driven her to pour out to him the whole story of what she knew was happening at No 53 Northbourne Park Villas at that moment. It had sustained her as he had taken her to the police-office and it had inspired her as she had repeated her tale to the Inspector there. And it had stayed with her while a sergeant and a party of constables had been gathered and had set out, with herself as guide, to help catch the despoilers of No 53 red-handed.

And it looked now as if, despite that well-known all-clear call, they had succeeded. With the first faint beginnings of day aiding the light of the sparse street-lamps, it was easily possible to make out, as they turned into the far end of Northbourne Park Villas, that the four-wheeler with the false plates was still standing there. But the all-clear had been given and the cab was ready to go. In a new spurt of rage she regretted piercingly that she had insisted on coming into the street from this end so as to avoid for as long as possible the sharp eyes of Old Henry. If they had come the other way they would have been within grabbing distance now.

And, yes –

'Look,' she cried. 'Look.'

The wide front door of No 53 had opened. And there he was. Val. Her Val. Not her Val. Carrying over each shoulder a large and bulging sack. A moment later there appeared behind him the tall figure of the Manchester Man with another sack over one shoulder and in the other hand the carpet-bag she herself had lugged all the way from Newel Street. And now Val was hurrying down the steps, those steps he had spoken to her of, where he had first met her. That Janey.

'Take him. Take him.'

The words broke from her, an abusive cry, sudden as a jagged sear of lightning in the daybreak silence.

'Take him.'

The shout was so sudden, so unexpected by the policemen beside her, that they none of them moved at all until along at the other end of the street the two creeping figures turned sharply towards them and then leapt the remainder of the steps in one bound and ran for the closed gate.

The shout, ringing in the stillness, had come too to the ears of the muffled-up cabbie sitting up on the waiting four-wheeler. Without stopping for the other two, he gave a hoarse shout and violently lashed out with his whip. The cab lurched and clattered away as if its horse had bolted.

At the gate Val and the Manchester Man both tried to pull the obstruction back at the same time. The Manchester Man shouldered Val aside in the end and went through ahead of him, letting his sack fall with a hollow clang but keeping tight hold of the carpet-bag. Val, too, dropped the sacks he had been carrying.

Beside Eileen the police party had by now woken to life. In a body they set out along the greyly sleeping street, boots banging out on the cobbles.

Eileen stood letting them go. Then, away at the house,

she saw one of the big windows on the second floor being pushed sharply up. The squeal of the cords came clearly to her. From out of it a figure appeared, white night-capped, white night-gowned. And a moment later there came the crack of a pistol shot. And then another.

The sound reversed in an instant all the feelings that had possessed her.

'Val,' she burst out. 'Val.'

From that second she loved him again, passionately and completely. His hopes were hers once more. Whatever he wanted, good or bad, within the law or without, was what she wanted. His purposes were hers. His enemies were hers, to the end.

She launched herself forward in the wake of the pounding police party, peering and straining into the distance in the quarter-light to see if she could make out what the pistol shots had done.

Both the fleeing men were running hard away along the street that led off at an angle from Northbourne Park Villas. But the old four-wheeler ahead of them was going faster. The police party seemed to be neither gaining nor losing ground. One of the group, in useless excitement, sprang his rattle adding its hideous noise to the pounding clatter of boots on cobbles.

Then as she ran and strained, some notion in her mind of catching hold of the police pursuers and somehow throwing them to the ground, she saw the tall Manchester Man drop the carpet-bag. The action sent fear clutching at her. She had been told so often by Noll Sproggs how valuable the bag's contents were. To see someone as formidable as the Manchester Man let it go made her realize as nothing else the extremity of the danger for the two fugitives, now momentarily out of sight.

But, coming to the end of Northbourne Park Villas and seeing the whole long chase again, she found the situation was worse for her than she had feared. Freed of his burden, the Manchester Man was now making much better speed than Val. For a moment she felt only rage at this. Why should he happen to be the better runner? Then something in Val's way of running told her that it was not because he was less fast that he was lagging: it was something else. Both of the pistol shots had not, as it had seemed at first, gone wide. One must have hit Val.

'No,' she called out in passionate rejection to the still clouded heavens. 'No.'

On she ran, sick half with effort half with fear. And on ahead of her, and drawing away, ran the burly uniformed policemen. And away in front the Manchester Man caught up with the swaying swinging cab, its driver standing up and using his long whip like a wild man. She saw the tall figure put out an arm and grab the cab's side. For a few paces he ran beside it. Then, with a leap that made the whole vehicle swing yet more to the side, he got himself on board.

But Val? He was impossibly far behind. The thundering policemen were nearer to him than he was to the cab. She could see clearly too that he was running clutching at his side. It was there that he must have been hit.

She ran onwards blindly. Her mind was full of one thing and one thing only, her image of Val. She felt as if she were him, that she was in him and of him, in every part and fibre of him. The sense of sharing, of merging, urged her forward at a speed she would never otherwise have been capable of.

She caught up with the policemen and pushed her way through. And then she saw that the cab, urged on no doubt by the power of its new passenger's will, was making even better speed than before. Already it was much further ahead, and, as she watched, it turned a corner and the distant sound of its horse's wildly clattering hooves faded from hearing. The Manchester Man had escaped. But his success only showed how much worse Val's plight was.

He was slowing visibly now, bending more and more to the left as he ran. And the policemen beside her were pounding along at a terrible swinging steady pace.

Then the sound of those thumping hobnail boots must have come plainly to Val's ears. He gave one long look behind him. Then he turned and, straightening his body, lunged forward almost twice as fast.

But it did not last. After thirty or forty paces at most he suddenly leant even more heavily than before to his left. But he staggered on.

Eileen even put her hand on to the arm of the police pursuer nearest to her as if about to try to bring to reality her fantasy of throwing the hunters one by one to earth. But the steadily running man did not seem even to notice.

Then, ahead, with a quickness Eileen wildly applauded, Val dodged round a corner that he had seemed to be entirely unaware of as he had approached it.

He'll do it, she shouted to herself in a blazing access of hope. If he can dodge he can do it. He's still far enough ahead.

She looked round trying, for the time it took to cover fifteen yards of roadway, to work out just where the chase had led them. But her knowledge of the neighbourhood, learnt only in her night of rage-filled wandering, was beyond telling her even remotely where she was, let alone whether there might be enough side-turnings and by-ways near for Val successfully to get away.

But one new hopeful thought did penetrate her mind. It was plain that the police party was not much more knowledgeable about the immediate area than she was herself. This was not their beat: it was Policeman Watson's and only he knew it really well.

Now the whole party of them rounded the corner of the street which Val had dodged into. They only just glimpsed him. He must have made another tremendous effort and put on a good turn of speed. He had passed a first turning and had just reached a second. Eileen felt a dart of pure pain. If only they had been a second or two slower. Then they were bound to have guessed he had seized on the nearer turning and he might well have succeeded in going to ground while they were on the false scent.

But it seemed that despite this piece of ill-luck Val had not been altogether deserted by the fates. When they turned the corner he had taken he was nowhere to be seen ahead of them.

It was only a short street and evidently he had reached the end of it. And there, glory be, were turnings to right and to left. And, when they came to these, once more there was no sign of the fugitive.

They came to a clattering halt. Puffing and groaning like a great walrus, the sergeant in charge gasped out some orders.

'He'll have slipped into hiding. Each one o' yer go a different way. We'll find him soon enough.'

And, hands on knees getting back his breath, he puffed out directions to each man in turn. In less than two minutes, breathing heavily and walking stiffly, they had set out.

Eileen stayed where she was.

What difference would it make which of them she

followed? She felt an overwhelming paradoxical onrush of despair. One of the hunters was bound to find Val. He might have hit on somewhere to hide himself, for a few minutes, but they had only to keep on looking. And there were so many of them. Sooner or later, just by going into every nook there was ahead, they would come across him. There were too many of them for Val to have luck on his side.

Wearily she leant against the railings of the corner house. The shouts and calls of the searchers grew more distant. Should she go home? At least she would not then see Val in handcuffs on his eventual way to transportation.

She looked round her to see which direction she had better set off in. And as she did so she recognised in the fast flooding-in daylight just exactly where she was.

She was in the very street where she had met Val at the start of this terrible night; just back from her was that accursed passageway where she had heard Policeman Watson utter the words that had turned her world upside-down. But what did what she had learnt there matter now? Val was wounded, hunted, on the very point of being taken and –

And then the notion came to her. Hadn't they all gone running hard past the entrance to that narrow passage? But had Val? Wasn't it possible that he had dodged down there neatly as he had dodged round the first corner?

She turned and hurried back, walking on tiptoe, fearful of letting anyone know where she was going. She reached the entrance to the passage. The daylight had hardly yet penetrated between its two high narrowly-separated walls. She glanced up and down the street. No one. She darted in.

'Val?' she called softly. 'Val?'

And from the far end of the passageway there came

an answer. It was a groan more than a call. But it was an answer. She ran forward.

Val was leaning against the locked gate at the far end. His face was white as cold ash. She raced to him and took him in her arms.

Policeman Watson, No 126, thinking of the near end of his spell of duty and pushing away an unpleasant suspicion that he ought to have gone back and looked into a deal of noise that he had heard some time earlier at the far end of his beat, turned the corner. And there, just vanishing into the very passageway where he had had that unfortunate encounter at the start of the night, was a whisk of female skirts.

And, blow me, he thought, if they don't look just like those coster-lass's. Could it be? What if she had returned to the scene of — To the scene. What if, after all, she was sorry for the way she had run off? Repentant. Coming back to confess she had been wrong, and to accept whatever chastisement . . .

He increased his pace and turned in at the entrance to the passage. He hurried down it, boots beating out on the paving-stones.

Val, almost beyond thinking, only half knowing it was Eileen there miraculously tending him, feeling the weakness grow in him with every passing second, heard like a bugle of alarm the thump of heavy boots coming inexorably down towards them. He broke from Eileen's arms and set himself, like a puling crab, to climb the smooth wall beside the locked gate.

Policeman Watson knew at once that here was a fellow

that ought to be taken in. But the blood seeping through
the fustian of his coat told him more than that. It told him
that here was a criminal who was dangerous. If the fellow
had been wounded, he was likely to wound in his turn.
And the girl was with him. There was one who should
never be trusted.

From his belt he drew his heavy rattle. He lifted it
high. He swung it hard. The clacking alarm spread out into
the morning air.

In a surprisingly short time it was answered by the
sound of running boots and three or four fellow-constables
headed by the sergeant from the police-office came hurrying down the passage.

Policeman Watson stood flat against one of the walls to
let the sergeant get at the fellow.

But when the sergeant came up he turned sharply
round to him.

'Here, Watson,' he said. 'This man's in a bad way. Is
there a surgeon living anywhere near? Knock him up
straight away, or we'll have a stiff 'un on our hands.'

Policeman Watson set off at a trot. What a night. What
a cursed unlucky night.

The surgeon, some twenty or thirty minutes later, looked
up from the body he had been bandaging where it lay on
the paving-stones of the narrow passageway.

'Well done, No 126,' he said to Policeman Watson, 'if
you hadn't had the foresight to come to me, this wretched
chap would have bled to death by now.'

Eileen, standing at the entrance to the passageway, a
heavyweight policeman on either side of her, heard them
coming out with Val. As they carried him past he opened

his eyes. For a moment he looked at her and then he murmured something.

The words were hard to catch, but she heard them.

'Girl, there's times, do what a man may, when chance is too strong fer anyone ter beat.'

Night falls on the battlefield. The dead and the dying lie where the hazard of battle felled them, those who did bravely and the cover-crawling cowards, the prudent and the rash, the poltroons and the energetically cunning. A lonely picquet, its riders counting themselves doubly fortunate at this hour, makes its way warily through the scene of carnage, alert for any chance sign that a combatant, friend or foe, may yet be saved. The reek of battle lingers in the air, tomorrow to be dissipated.